"Charlie h[...]
he will at the ball," Emma said [...]

"This is an arrangement, then?" Francesca asked.

"Not precisely," Emma admitted. "Charlie isn't *obliged* to offer for me, but it has been an understanding in the family for years."

"We do the same in Spain. I was arranged to marry a friend of my father's, but I did not eat for three days," Francesca confided. "And what about you, Elizabeth? Do you have an arrangement?"

"No indeed," Elizabeth avowed with a shudder. "I plan to follow the English custom and marry for love."

"Lord Westbridge, perhaps?" Francesca asked with a knowing smile.

Emma was overcome with amusement. "Oh, Francesca, where did you get *that* idea? I plan to introduce him to *you*."

"We will see," Francesca said diplomatically. "There is certainly more than one lord in England—enough for all, I should think."

Or was there?

# Distant Relations

BY

## Denice Greenlea

FAWCETT COVENTRY  •  NEW YORK

Published by Fawcett Coventry Books, a unit of CBS
Publications, the Educational and Professional Pub-
lishing Division of CBS, Inc.

ISBN 0-449-50300-3

Printed in the United States of America

First Fawcett Coventry Edition: July 1982
10 9 8 7 6 5 4 3 2 1

## AUTHOR'S NOTE

The famous prizefighter of the late eighteenth and early nineteenth century, Daniel Mendoza, who was known as the Great Jew, did indeed have a fight with a tollkeeper in a town called Billingsgate. I have taken the liberty of changing the town's name to Budgate, so that I could place it where I pleased on the map of England and people it with characters of my invention.

# ONE

Elizabeth Durant was carefully plotting the best way to dispose permanently of her cousin, Emma Locke, as that young lady droned on and on, punctuating her remarks with suitable gestures, blithely unaware that her demise was being planned even as she spoke. Death from an overdose of laudanum would be expedient, Elizabeth thought, but too kind. To drift quietly off into deep, unending sleep was too easy a passing away for such an unremitting and unrepentant bore as Emma. Elizabeth had heard that the bells of St. Paul's were deadly should one stand too near them while they were being sounded. Death by cacophony seemed eminently suitable for one whose tongue never ceased to wag, clapperlike, in her mouth. Now the only thing left for Elizabeth to do was to figure out a way to lure her cousin to the belltower of St. Paul's.

Emma had barely paused for breath since the arrival of yet another cousin that afternoon. This visitor had been eagerly awaited for weeks, and the house had been cleaned from top to bottom as much in her honor as in anticipation of the beginning of this latest social season. Mrs. Locke had even thoughtfully provided an abundant supply of coals in the bedroom prepared for the visitor, with orders that a fire should be lit whenever it was so desired, even if the other residents of the household were sweltering. For this visitor was accustomed to a sunnier clime, and might find even a warm English spring cold compared to her native Spain.

Mr. Locke had been sent off in the carriage to the local posting inn in good time to collect the visitor and her baggage, although, mail coaches being what they were, he returned some minutes later than expected. Emma had been restlessly keeping watch at the drawing-room window, and was in a near frenzy of anticipation by the time the carriage finally pulled up at the door. She proclaimed the news importantly to her mother and Elizabeth, and they all busied themselves with their needlework as if that were their only concern of the day, so they would not appear too anxious or ill-bred to their cousin.

A few minutes later the butler opened the door and announced, "Miss Francesca DelSorro," and Mrs. Locke calmly put aside her sewing to rise and greet the girl warmly.

"My dear, we are so pleased to have you with us," she said, holding out her hands. "Welcome to London."

"You must be my cousin Annabel," Miss DelSorro replied, returning the embrace. "I am very pleased indeed to be here."

"And here are two more of your cousins, my dear. My daughter, Emma, and Elizabeth Durant."

Miss DelSorro bowed to each of them in turn, her movements graceful, her smile brilliant. Mr. Locke joined them shortly, after giving orders for the disposal of the carriage and the baggage, and the beaming grin on the face of this normally taciturn man indicated well his pleasure at receiving such a fine example of the Spanish aristocracy into his home. In fact, upon his first sight of Miss DelSorro, he had forgotten his previous misgivings about harboring a foreigner of Roman persuasion, and acted just as if he alone were responsible for her presence there.

Mrs. Locke then asked Miss DelSorro if she would like to see her room and freshen up before tea, and Francesca acquiesced most graciously. So the butler, who had been hovering in the doorway with Miss

DelSorro's maid, was called upon to lead the guest to her room. The maid followed behind, clutching a portmanteau and regarding everything about her with wide eyes.

Mrs. Locke sat down and again took up her needlework.

"Well, George," she said with a twinkle, "what do you think of my cousin *now?*" She had been well acquainted with her husband's objections on that score, and though she was a cheerful woman who had no idea how to hold a grudge, she could not resist indulging in at least one good-natured I-told-you-so.

"Very fine young lady, very fine indeed," he replied proudly.

It was then that Emma began talking. The first sight of her cousin had left her momentarily slack-jawed and silent, but as soon as the new arrival left the room, the dam burst.

"I have never seen a traveling suit cut in exactly that style," she bubbled enthusiastically. "What would you call that color, Mama? I should call it mulberry, I think. With all that black piping it appeared quite *military.* How should I look in a suit such as that, Mama? Did she have a great many boxes, Papa? Her wardrobe must be very fine. Of course, her complexion is rather dark for my taste—it is what is called olive, is it not, Mama? Elizabeth, I think she must be quite as tall as you are. She certainly appeared most *majestic* as she came through the door. I declare I was quite bowled over. And her *hair!* It is almost blue, it is so dark. I don't think I should care for hair like that myself, but then it does go with her complexion." She pushed a wisp of her own pale, curly hair out of her face as she paused for breath.

"And did you have the opportunity to count her teeth as well?" Elizabeth inquired wryly. "Her smile was quite broad enough."

Emma cast her a withering glance and continued in her admiration of her new cousin, so much more attractive to her for her very novelty. Indeed, her flow of chatter did not wane even when Francesca returned downstairs in yet another garment of interesting cut for tea, nor when tea was removed, nor did the brief interlude when it was time to change for dinner cause her to lose her place in her narrative. During dinner, Elizabeth did manage to put a remark in here and there, and Francesca even squeezed in a few monosyllabic replies. But Emma doggedly held on to her advantage and did not allow anyone else to lead the conversation for more than ten seconds.

After dinner, Mr. Locke left to look in at his club, and Mrs. Locke sat with the girls for a short time, before stating that she was off to bed and would let them all chatter without the dampening influence of an adult's presence. Emma had not noticed any such influence, and told her mother so as she kissed her affectionately goodnight. Mrs. Locke hugged the other two girls fondly and told Francesca again how happy she was to have her with them.

When her mother left, Emma picked up exactly where she had left off. She had already described to Francesca every room in the house and what furnishings she had had a hand in selecting, and had even given a brief description of the Lockes' country home as well. She had listed all the things Francesca would find to interest her in London, most of the people she would meet, and what kinds of entertainment she would enjoy, with some emphasis on Emma's own coming-out ball the following week. She had now advanced to describing, in intimate detail, the gown she would be wearing for that ball, and it was at this point that Elizabeth began to think of ways she might be permanently silenced. How could Emma go on and on about such mundane matters when all that they had discovered from their cousin was that she lived in Madrid and that her maid, who was called Conchita, did not speak any English? Elizabeth had a million questions to ask about Spain and Francesca's life there, not the

10

least of which was why she had decided to make this visit, and all Emma could do was chatter endlessly about gowns and draperies.

"And I wanted to have lots and lots of lace all around the edge of the neckline, too," Emma was saying, "but Mama said it would be too fussy. Simplicity, she told me, was best for one of my figure, so I decided upon a very narrow edging of Brussels lace, which I thought was the very thing."

She is too fat for anything else, Elizabeth thought unkindly, and indeed Emma might be called, even by the gentlest critic, pleasingly plump. However, she was young and had the pretty pink complexion that goes with youth. While in years to come she might tend toward the more obvious corpulence of her mother and father, at seventeen she was quite as pretty as she ever would be, with her flaxen hair, pale-blue eyes, and rounded cheeks with their healthy tint of rose.

Elizabeth, unfortunately, could not see her cousin in this light, for she remembered Emma too well as a spotty, pesky child of thirteen, while at fifteen Elizabeth was already blossoming into beauty. Elizabeth's coloring was a more intense version of her cousin's, her hair a deeper gold, her eyes a deeper blue. And while she might have had quite as much flesh as Emma, and even more, she was a good six inches taller than her cousin, and that flesh was distributed in longer, leaner curves. Perhaps the only thing marring her beauty at that moment was a look of extreme impatience.

Emma's endurance finally seemed to be flagging, and Francesca was able to insert a remark of her own. "You English girls have very fine complexions," she said. "I cannot wear the white dress at all." She turned her head toward Elizabeth, in an effort to include her in the conversation. "But tell me, are you also to be presented at this ball?"

Elizabeth smiled. "No, this will be my fourth season. I had my own ball three years ago."

"Ah, yes, so it is for me, too, but my first in England, of course." Francesca smiled back.

11

"Do they do it the same way in Spain?" Emma asked, distracted for the moment from the subject of gowns. "Did you have a large ball in your honor and a new dress and everything?"

"Yes, the ball, of course, but the dress—it is not so important. I always have the new dress." Francesca shrugged her shoulders slightly, then, fearing she might have offended Emma, added quickly, "But yours sounds most lovely."

Elizabeth gave Francesca an amused shake of her head—she knew Emma was not one to notice subtleties. "Tell me, cousin," she said, seizing the opportunity quickly before Emma went on to describe her undergarments as well, "how do you find England so far?"

Francesca shrugged again. "It is damp, but that I was warned of before I left Spain by my English grandmama. She, of course, finds Spain too dry, but has grown used to it. So far I have seen very little of the country, except from the window of the coach. It is very green—this, I think, is the thing that strikes one most. I look forward to meeting many English people."

"Oh, you certainly will do that!" Emma exclaimed. "Why, we have engagements for every night this week, and everyone is *dying* to meet you; they all know you are coming."

"Yes, you have told me so already," Francesca said. "It will be pleasant to meet a lot of people. It will help me to forget my lover whom I left behind." She gave the slightest suggestion of a sigh.

Elizabeth regarded her with renewed curiosity, while Emma's eyes opened wide.

"You left your lover behind!" Emma exclaimed. "How terrible for you!"

"No, not at all," Francesca said with a smile. "He was most unsuitable. That is why Papa has sent me here. Go to your English cousins, he told me, and learn from them how to behave, and so I come. Yes, Papa, I said to him, that seems to me a good idea, and perhaps

12

I may meet an English lord while I am here. He thought that was an excellent idea." Then she added, as though inquiring about the best shops, "Do you know of any English lords I might marry?"

"You are certain to meet Lord Westbridge tomorrow," Emma said, proud that she could produce a peer on such short notice. "We are attending a musical evening at Lady Imogen Waters' and he is her brother and so is bound to be there."

The mention of Lord Westbridge's name produced an interesting effect in both the other young ladies. Francesca straightened up from the languid pose she had fallen into while Emma was talking, and Elizabeth regarded her folded hands intently, as a slight flush crept over her face. Francesca, who unlike Emma was always keenly aware of subtleties, noticed this at once.

"I believe I am already acquainted with this Lord Westbridge," Francesca said, keeping one eye on Elizabeth to note any further reaction.

Elizabeth looked at her quickly, then looked down again.

"How wonderful!" Emma said enthusiastically. "Where did you meet him?"

"If it is the same gentleman, I knew him during the occupation. We were occupied by many English troops in Madrid toward the end of the war there. They were all very dashing and taught me much English. Is this Lord Westbridge a military man?"

"Yes, I believe he served on the Peninsula," Elizabeth said quietly.

"How very delightful!" Francesca said. "I will be most pleased to meet El Colonel again." She pronounced the word as it was spelled. "You are acquainted with him, too, Elizabeth?" She already knew the answer to this question, and Elizabeth merely affirmed it.

"We have stood up together on several occasions," Elizabeth admitted offhandedly.

Francesca's brow creased. "Stood up? What is that? In Spain we dance together; it is much more pleasant."

Emma laughed, a loud, unattractive bray that came ill out of her doll-like mouth and that her mother had been trying to cure her of for years. "That is what 'stand up' means—to dance together. But cousin," she went on and leaned toward her confidentially, "you must be certain not to stand up with any man more than twice. It would be most improper to do so, unless you are engaged."

"I see," Francesca said gravely. "Thank you for telling me that. That must be what Papa meant when he said you would teach me to behave. In Spain I stood up, as you say, with no one but Hernando, and that is why I am here." She gave a brief sigh. "I must not make the same mistake again. I should not like to return to Spain too soon."

"Certainly not! That would be dreadful!" Emma declared. "You must remain with us for ever and ever, and tomorrow we will introduce you to Lord Westbridge. Of course, there will be positively *dozens* of lords at my ball"—this with some smug pride—"but I think Lord Westbridge is among the best. He will be a duke someday."

"A duke? That is a very fine thing indeed," Francesca said, and she did not miss the dagger glances that Elizabeth cast at Emma. "But perhaps it would be best if I stood up with him only once, even though we are old friends. That is suitable, is it not?"

"Yes, of course," Emma assured her, "but there won't be any dancing tomorrow night—I am not allowed to attend a dancing evening until after my ball. It will be a musical evening only, with refreshments afterwards."

"Not allowed to dance until after your ball?" Francesca asked. "That is very interesting. Perhaps I should write these things down, or I will forget them. I will send Conchita out for a memorandum book tomorrow; it will give her a chance to learn the city. But tell me, how do you learn to dance if you cannot dance until after your ball?"

Again Emma laughed loudly. "Oh, I know how to dance—I have had a dancing master, of course, and

14

have been to several dancing parties in the country, where it doesn't count. It is only that I am not allowed to dance in public until I am out."

Francesca's brow creased. "Out where? This I do not understand."

Emma explained after another snort of laughter, and Francesca said, "It is a very strange language, this English. I thought I spoke it well, but it appears I do not."

"You speak it beautifully!" Emma gushed. "One hardly notices your accent. It will simply take some time for you to learn all the little funny bits."

"I thought I had learned all the funny bits from the English soldiers," Francesca said. "Of course, I have not had much opportunity to practice them, and Grandmama used to turn quite blue when I repeated to her the words the soldiers taught me." She caught Elizabeth's eye, and they shared a look of amusement.

"We will be glad to help you along," Elizabeth put in, but before she had a chance to lead the conversation firmly away from any further mention of Lord Westbridge and ask Francesca about her sea journey, Emma launched into a long explanation of the other events they had planned that week. This took some time, as she named each activity in no particular order and had to repeat herself several times to make it clear to her cousin which day was meant.

"And tomorrow Charlie promised to come and take us all driving in the park," she said. "I think I told you that before, but I didn't mention that you must be very careful about whom you are seen with in the park. If you receive an invitation from a gentleman, it would be best to check with my father first and make sure he is a suitable *parti* or there will be the most dreadful scandal."

"Thank you for telling me that," Francesca said. "But again I am confused. Would I not tell your mother, as she must come along as duenna?"

Emma regarded her blankly, stopped short by this

15

completely unfamiliar word and the absolute absurdity of bringing her mother along on a drive.

"I am sorry, I do not know the English," Francesca said, appealing to Elizabeth.

" 'Chaperon' would be the correct word, I believe," Elizabeth told her, "although I do not believe it has quite the same connotations. A suitable chaperon, in some circumstances, can be a maid or a groom, while a duenna is always a respectable elder female relation, is she not?"

Francesca nodded. "So despite all your rules, you English girls actually have more freedom than we in Spain," she said. "Although my duenna, Tia Rosa, who is my father's elder sister, could always be depended upon to fall asleep after two glasses of Madeira, a circumstance Hernando and I often took advantage of. I don't suppose one usually gives Madeira to grooms or maids? No, I thought not. I am sure it would take much more than that to put Conchita to sleep." She turned back to Emma. "Now this Charlie you mentioned, who is he? He is, I take it, a suitable *parti*, entirely approved by your father? I should not like to damage my reputation my first day here."

"Oh, yes, of course," Emma assured her. "He is my cousin on my mother's side, so he is not really related to you or Elizabeth, although Elizabeth's father was his guardian until he reached the age of one and twenty. Did I not tell you of him before? My mother was a Buckley and her brother, Walter, was Charlie's father, but he died when Charlie was little, or my Uncle Gerald would not have been his guardian. We are to be married, probably."

"You and your Uncle Gerald?" Francesca asked, surprised. "That is unusual. I did not know it was permitted by the English church. It sounds a much more liberal faith than Grandmama led me to believe."

Emma brayed. "No—I am to marry my cousin Charlie. It is quite all right for cousins to marry. Besides, Uncle Gerald has just recently married someone else, and Elizabeth has a new stepmama who is only a few

16

years older than she, isn't that right, Lizzie?" She paused briefly, to allow Elizabeth time for a nod. "Of course, Charlie has not yet asked me, but most likely he will at my ball, and then we can announce it that same night. I am looking forward to it exceedingly."

"This is an arrangement, then?" Francesca asked. "That is very sensible. I was arranged to marry a friend of my father's, but I did not eat for three days, and that is another reason I am here. But I thought you didn't have such things in England. Grandmama told me the English always marry for love, which is how she was allowed to marry my grandfather."

"It is not precisely an arrangment," Emma admitted. "I mean, Charlie isn't *obliged* to offer for me, but there has been an understanding about it in the family ever since we were little. You see, my mother inherited some of my grandfather's estate and Charlie has the rest, so it makes sense that we should marry and put it back together again."

"We do the same in Spain," Francesca said approvingly. "And what about you, Elizabeth? Do you have such an arrangement, too?"

"No, indeed," Elizabeth avowed with a shudder. "*I* plan to follow the English custom and marry for love."

"Lord Westbridge, perhaps?" Francesca asked with a knowing smile, and Elizabeth flushed again but did not deny it.

Emma was overcome with amusement at this idea, and her horsy laugh effectively curtailed all conversation until she had recovered. "Lord Westbridge and Elizabeth? Oh, Francesca, where did you get *that* idea? I told you I would introduce him to *you*."

Elizabeth said nothing, but was mentally perfecting her plan to lure Emma atop St. Paul's.

"We will see," Francesca said diplomatically. "There is certainly more than one lord in England—enough for all, I should think."

Elizabeth cast her a grateful glance as Emma took the brief ensuing silence as an opportunity to launch into yet another monologue, describing in detail all the lords she could think of that might interest Francesca. But before she could name more than three, Francesca interrupted her.

"I am bored with that now," she said. "I think I am having the headache, if you will excuse me." It had not taken her long to learn that Emma was impervious to hints and that the only thing that would stop the flow of words was a blunt, direct statement.

Emma was immediately contrite and apologized profusely to her cousin. "I am so sorry, Cousin Francesca, I had forgotten how tired you must be after your journey, and we have already kept you up quite late with our gossip and chatter. Mama is always telling me—"

"I will go to bed now," Francesca interrupted again. "I am sure we will talk again tomorrow. Elizabeth, if you like I will tell you several amusing stories about Lord Westbridge, and then you can do the same for me when I meet someone I am interested in."

Elizabeth returned her smile warmly, for she realized that Francesca was telling her quite plainly that she had no intention of presuming on her old friendship with Lord Westbridge and cutting Elizabeth out. From that moment she knew she would get on well with her new cousin, while her old cousin decidedly needed to be taken down a notch or two.

As soon as Francesca had left them, Elizabeth turned roundly on Emma.

"Really, Emma, you might show more sensitivity. Poor Francesca has been yawning this half hour past—anyone with an ounce of sense could see she was longing for her bed."

"I told her I was sorry," Emma pouted, then brightened again. "But isn't it funny that she thinks you and Lord Westbridge have some sort of arrangement? I wonder what could have given her such an idea."

"You were obviously not following the conversation carefully, Emma," Elizabeth said, folding her needlework, which had lain untouched beside her this whole time, and placing it back into her work box. "I said I

18

planned to marry for love, and Francesca suggested Lord Westbridge might be the object of my affection."

Emma brayed. "That is exactly what I mean—it is too funny for words."

"I do not agree with you in the least," Elizabeth said coldly, rising and heading for the door.

"Lizzie, don't tell me you have a *tendre* for Lord Westbridge! Oh, that is a funny bit of news!" Emma crowed.

Elizabeth's jaw tightened. "Emma, you are coming dangerously close to having your hair pulled, just as when we were little."

"Well, I am sure it doesn't make the least difference to me," Emma said airily, putting her own things away. "After all, I have Charlie and I am a good deal more sure of him than you are of Lord Westbridge—and you in your fourth season, too."

As she had intended, Emma's arrow found its mark, for this was indeed a sore point with Elizabeth. Her fourth season and not yet married! Soon she would stop receiving proposals altogether, and then where would she be? Firmly planted on the shelf, wearing little white lace caps, and knitting booties for the ungainly offspring of Emma and Charles Buckley. But was it her fault she had loved none of the gentlemen who had offered for her? Even if she had to wait through two more seasons, Elizabeth was determined she would marry for love.

"Personally," Elizabeth said haughtily, "I can think of nothing more depressing than to marry someone like Charles Buckley, a man—a *boy* we have both known all of our lives, someone who rarely takes his nose out of a book long enough to give one the time of day. And he is a terrible dancer," she added, the most scathing indictment of all. "Where's the romance in marrying someone like that?"

"Who gives two figs for romance?" Emma said with a sniff. "*I* can think of nothing more depressing than to be left on the shelf." And if Emma had only been a little younger, she might have stuck out her tongue.

19

Unfortunately, Elizabeth could think of no rejoinder besides a childish "And I'll wager Charlie will never offer for you, so there," which she did not utter as it probably was not true. Charlie was one of those boring young men who would probably do his duty. So instead, she uttered a cold "Goodnight," and left her cousin alone.

# TWO

Charles Buckley sat in the reading lounge of the Socrates Club, and as his cousin had predicted he had his nose in a book. At the moment, he was not alone in his pursuit, for several other gentlemen present there were similarly occupied. Indeed, the Socrates Club had been founded as a gathering place for those who wished to enlarge their philosophical knowledge by reading all the latest books on the subject in the reading lounge, or engaging in discussions of the same in the pompously titled Socratic Dialogue Lounge. There was also a dining room, which served up quite a respectable mixed grill and black pudding and boasted an even more respectable wine list whenever members felt the need to supplement the nourishment of the mind with the nourishment of the body. The rooms were decorated in subdued shades of burgundy and moss green, as these colors were thought to be conducive to deep and serious thought, and the carpets were thick and soft to absorb any distracting footsteps. Mr. Buckley had come to the club with a letter of introduction from his friend Richard Tanner, and as an Oxonian with a most respectable background of breeding and modest wealth, had been quickly and easily accepted as a member.

Mr. Buckley appeared an exceedingly studious gentleman as he sat there, an impressive volume bound in red morocco on his lap, a pair of spectacles slipping down his nose. He was not unpersonable, however; his features were strong and attractive, his fair hair cut in the latest fashion, his eyes a deep, clear blue. His well-tailored and obviously new suit of clothing covered what appeared to be a quite muscular body, although that might have been no more than clever padding. Indeed, the only defects in his person were a lack of height and a set of chewed-off fingernails, the result of a habit he had been trying to break himself of since childhood.

He was chewing one of those fingernails now, the index finger of his right hand, to be precise, and while he paused in this activity at regular intervals to turn the page, he was not really taking in what he was reading. He cast frequent, surreptitious glances about the room from time to time, in the hopes that one of his fellow readers might be inclined to put aside his volume and engage in conversation—or even dialogue— instead, but they all remained irritatingly intent and did not notice Mr. Buckley's restlessness. He felt very much inclined to summon paper and pen and write to Richard Tanner to tell him that he did not find the Socrates Club a great meeting place as promised, nor had he made the acquaintance of a vast number of men who shared his tastes and interests, as Mr. Tanner represented he would.

Perhaps Mr. Buckley could be forgiven for not entering into the studious spirit of the Socrates Club, for although he was quite three-and-twenty, this was his first season in London and he was more than eager for some livelier entertainment. He had visited the metropolis, of course, on many previous occasions, and even owned a house in town, which was let to a quiet and respectable dowager who could be depended upon not to spoil too many rooms with wallpaper of an Egyptian persuasion. But while he had enjoyed Oxford, indeed had remained there an extra year to read history, he was now ready for a taste of the "real world," just to see how he liked it. He was looking forward to sampling the "social whirl" he had heard so much of from his relations. He had even given some thought to the possibility of romance, for while he already knew the girl he wished to marry, had known her since childhood, he had not totally eliminated the possibility of meeting someone even more to his liking. The trouble was in obtaining invitations and introductions, and while the Socrates Club had seemed a good place to begin, he was clearly making no progress in that direction this morning. With a sigh, he turned another page.

Thus Mr. Buckley experienced no displeasure at all when he was interrupted from his labor by hearing his name spoken. He closed his book readily, not bothering to mark his place, and looked up to see an extraordinarily handsome young man approaching him.

"Charles Buckley! I thought I recognized you!"

Charles rose to grasp his extended hand, unable for the moment to recall his name or the circumstances under which they had met before. Certainly, Charles knew the gentleman, for one rarely encountered a face and figure of such classical Grecian beauty and was unlikely to forget it if one had.

"Foxmoor," the amiable gentleman supplied. "Nigel Foxmoor. We met at your uncle's wedding last summer."

"Yes, of course," Charles said. "Foxmoor! Good to see you again. Won't you join me?"

Several of the other readers in the room looked up in annoyance at the disturbance, and Charles lowered his voice to ask Mr. Foxmoor to join him in the dialogue lounge.

"Whew!" Mr. Foxmoor said with expression when they had settled themselves and placed an order for refreshments with the waiter. "I had forgotten what a dashed stodgy place this was! Just came from White's, you know, and it was too noisy there and I didn't see a soul I knew, so I thought I would just pop round to my other clubs, and lucky I did!" He glanced around the room, apparently examining the furnishings. "Thought they would have changed those draperies by now.

23

Haven't been here in years—prefer to do my reading in the comfort of my own home."

The waiter brought their drinks, and Mr. Foxmoor took a sip and then said, "This is my first day back in town, and you are the first person I've seen, so tell me how the season seems to be shaping up so far."

Charles pushed his spectacles up reflectively, not quite certain what information was required by that question. "It seems to be shaping up well," he offered tentatively. "Of course, I have nothing to compare it with, as this is my first season in this city."

"Is it indeed?" Nigel exclaimed. "Of course—it was in Bath that we met. Lovely city—I've spent quite a bit of time there myself, but now it holds painful memories for me." This was uttered in quite a cheerful tone of voice.

"I'm so sorry," Charlie murmured. He did not know Mr. Foxmoor well and did not wish to presume on such a brief acquaintance by asking personal questions.

"Not at all! Not at all!" Nigel assured him. "When one loves, one must always be prepared for the possibility of disappointment, you know."

"Yes, I suppose that is very true," Charlie agreed, for it was.

"Of course, some good has come of it, too," Nigel continued. "For if I had not loved the lady, I would not have been invited to her wedding, and then I would not have met you there and I would not have known you when I walked in here ten minutes ago, and I would still be wandering about London, lonely and alone. Funny thing, life."

"It certainly is," Charlie agreed, although he had had some trouble following this chain of reasoning.

"Yes, it is," Nigel added for good measure. "It is always teaching you something, too. My great lesson was that it is not the worst thing to have loved and lost, for one can always love again." He appeared to be quite proud of this axiom of his own invention.

"Quite," Charles said, smiling. He found he liked Mr. Foxmoor, and appreciated the easy, unpretentious manner in which he revealed his confidences, as if he had known Charles a long time instead of having met him only once before.

"The point of the matter is," Nigel continued, "even though the lady in question and I shouldn't have suited, I cannot help believing that there must be some other lady in this great city who should suit, don't you know?"

"Of course," Charles agreed. "It is a populous city."

"Exactly!" Nigel said enthusiastically. "You see, the notion has taken a hold on me. I used to be quite opposed to the idea, you know. Was always turning tail and running whenever the danger seemed imminent. But in recent months I have been able to concentrate on little else but the desire to be comfortably wed, and I am not getting any younger, which is plain to see, so I have come to London to find myself a wife."

Charles smiled. "You have come to wive it wealthily in Padua."

Nigel regarded him with slight confusion. "Yes, a wealthy wife would not be amiss, although it is not entirely necessary, as I am plump enough in the pockets myself. But where is Padua? Should I know about it? Is is similar to Almack's?"

"No," Charles said, politely suppressing a laugh. "I was merely quoting—Shakespeare, you know."

"Oh, I see. I'm not much of a one for Shakespeare, myself. If the truth must be known I rather prefer more modern fare. In fact"—he glanced around and lowered his voice in preparation for the revelation of a dark secret—"I am rather fond of the Gothic, you know— lots of blood and guts and damsels in distress, that sort of thing."

"There is nothing to be ashamed of in that," Charles reassured him. "You are not the only one who enjoys that guilty pleasure. Why, if all those who claimed they never read novels were telling the truth, the things would never be written in the first place, and certainly would not sell in vast enough quantities for publishers to take the trouble of printing them."

"There you have it!" Nigel said, pleased. "Then I don't mind telling you I find Shakespeare and those chaps dashed dull. A good novel full of excitement and adventure and love is much more to my liking."

"Then you must have read this new book that is making a sensation—the one by Mary Shelley. It is much as you describe."

"Yes, indeed!" Nigel exclaimed. "The very thing. Affected me very deeply, I can tell you. In fact, it was that book that finally convinced me I needed a wife."

"How do you mean?" Charlie wondered.

"Well, that poor brute in the book, all he wanted was a wife; if he had found himself a nice little woman to settle down with—or if that Frankenstein chap had made him a wife as he promised—things might have turned out quite differently for him. And here I am, in the same predicament. Although I don't think I would fancy a patchwork sort of lady," he added reflectively. "One of the ordinary sort will do quite nicely."

Charles nodded agreement, for while he saw little the handsome gentleman before him might have in common with Mary Shelley's horrible creature, he did not think a patchwork wife would suit his fancy, either.

"And have you had any success yet?" Charles inquired. "I mean, have you met any young lady—of the usual variety—you would care to marry?"

"Early days yet, early days," Nigel said. "As I told you, I arrived in London but last night and have had no chance to let all my old acquaintances know my direction, so I haven't received any invitations yet. But there is plenty of time; the season has hardly begun."

"Indeed," Charles agreed, then brightened as he saw how he might help Nigel along. "Look here, I am engaged to drive out with my cousins this afternoon—why don't you join us?"

"Cousins? What sort of cousins?" Nigel asked.

"Three of them, all of one piece and all quite eligible young ladies. One has not been presented yet, but will be next week, and I am sure she will be happy to extend to you an invitation to her ball. Then there

26

is my Uncle Gerald's daughter, Elizabeth Durant. You may be acquainted with her already."

Nigel pondered for a moment. "Lovely tall girl with a mass of golden hair?" he asked.

"Yes, that is she," Charles affirmed.

"Ah, a splendid creature. I recall being quite taken with her."

Charles made no reply to this, but added rather quickly, "And then there is a third cousin, whom I haven't met. She is visiting from Spain."

Nigel was quite enlivened by this information. "Spanish, eh? That sounds dashed interesting. Lots of castles in Spain, or so one would gather from all the books. Do you think she lives in a castle? A noble lady from Castile, dark of hair, olive of skin."

From the change in his voice Charles assumed Nigel was quoting and politely allowed him to finish.

"I don't know about the castle," Charles said with a crooked smile. "Perhaps you would care to ask her about it yourself."

"Don't mind if I do! Splendid of you, asking me along. You are quite sure they won't mind?"

"Not at all. They will probably be pleased that I have brought someone new along." He gave a slightly rueful smile. "I am due there at two, and in the meantime I had planned to take luncheon here and then go over to Gentleman Jackson's for a few rounds."

"Ah, you're a follower of the fancy," Nigel said knowingly. "I mean no offense, but I would not have guessed by looking at you."

"That is why I learned to defend myself when I was in school," Charlie told him, pushing his spectacles up with one finger. "It is one of the few things I do well. I'm not much of a hand with horses and I haven't the eye for fencing or shooting."

"We must meet for some sparring sometime," Nigel said amiably. "Though I am not very good myself. Only took it up because it was the fashion. But horses—now there is something I know a bit about. In fact, I don't know what your turnout is like, but at the risk of

27

sounding immodest I'll wager it can't hold a candle to mine. I've just purchased a spanking pair of blacks, each with four white stockings. Not long-distance-goers, you understand—couldn't be with those white feet—but splendid steppers nonetheless and perfect for a drive in the park. Bought myself a new carriage, too—lovely shade of yellow, with black trim. What do you say I collect you and your three ladies in my rig at two, and we'll turn some heads, I can tell you, if the ladies are as fine as the horses."

Charles could have told him that at least one of the ladies would easily outshine any horse and carriage, however fine, but he merely said that the plan was perfectly agreeable to him and gave Nigel the Lockes' direction on Upper Grosvenor Street, promising to meet him there promptly at two.

It would seem that Francesca DelSorro owned no item of clothing that was duller than cherry red, and undoubtedly the brilliant color of her driving ensemble, with its black braiding and Spanish cut, suited her swarthy complexion perfectly. Elizabeth suddenly felt as showy as a wren when she joined her cousin in the drawing room and viewed her in all her splendor. But Francesca's eye for the dramatic was not confined to the adornment of her own person. She immediately exclaimed to Elizabeth:

"The two of us, you and I, we must be sure to always wear gowns of complementing colors, for then when we stand next to each other there will be no one in the room who will be able to look elsewhere." She put her arm around Elizabeth's waist and led her to the large mirror overhanging the mantelpiece to demonstrate what she meant.

Indeed, they did make a striking portrait. Elizabeth's own driving outfit of deep blue was most pleasing next to Francesca's red, and the shining gold of her hair was emphasized by the blue-black of Francesca's, instead of appearing washed-out as she had feared.

Elizabeth laughed happily. "Yes, we do look rather nice together."

"We look *glorious*," Francesca assured her gravely.

The picture they made together was not lost on Emma either, when she entered in her own pale-yellow gown, which was quite pretty but quite ordinary to her thinking. If only her mother would allow her to choose her own clothes, she thought sulkily when she saw her two cousins posing together. As soon as she was married to Charlie she would buy herself dozens of new frocks, all of them red or orange or purple, or some combination thereof.

Mrs. Locke was happily unaware of her daughter's tasteless longings when she ambled in a few minutes later to cluck happily over her girls before they left on their outing.

"You all look quite lovely," she said, including her daughter wholeheartedly in this compliment. "Elizabeth, my dear, do be sure to keep your parasol up; you know you have a tendency to freckle. Emma, darling, don't slouch, it spoils the line of your dress. Francesca, I do hope you enjoy the drive and do not find it too cold here."

They heard the jingle of the doorbell, and Mrs. Locke, adjusting a flounce on her daughter's bodice, reminded her once more not to chew on the ends of her gloves, for it was very distressing to see the tips of her fingers always poking out through the holes and might cause people to think that she could not afford a new pair. Emma acquiesced with a sigh and turned to greet Charlie with something less than the enthusiasm one might expect from a girl greeting her future husband, but then she was concentrating on not slouching or chewing and so might be excused.

All the ladies might be excused for a mild degree of rudeness when they saw the young Adonis who followed Charles into the room. Introductions were quickly made, and Charlie explained that Nigel had very kindly offered to drive them all himself.

"Mr. Foxmoor, how very pleasant to see you again,"

Elizabeth said, smiling. "It was in Brighton that we met last, was it not?"

"No, it was at your father's wedding in Bath," he corrected her. "I was a friend of the bride, you may recall."

"I certainly do," she replied, "and I was always exceedingly jealous of Anna, for whenever she was around, you paid very little attention to *me*."

"A circumstance I will attempt to remedy," he said gallantly.

"Foxmoor?" Mrs. Locke repeated. "My husband's mother was a Foxmoor. I wonder if they could be the same ones. Let me see, her father was a Sidney Foxmoor, from Devon."

"The very ones!" Nigel exclaimed happily. "Sidney Foxmoor was my great-uncle."

Mrs. Locke was pleased. "Then you are related to all three of my girls, for Sidney Foxmoor was great-grandfather to them all."

"But I am confused," Francesca put in. "I thought Mr. Buckley was our cousin, not Mr. Foxmoor."

"Actually, Charlie is my brother's son," Mrs. Locke explained, "and therefore Mr. Foxmoor is more closely related to you and Elizabeth."

"As long as it is not close enough to make idiots," Francesca said, smiling provocatively at Nigel.

Charles laughed, while Nigel looked perplexed.

"I do not think you need to worry about that, Miss DelSorro," Charles said. "We are all quite distant relations, except for Emma and me—we are first cousins."

"Then you will have the idiots," Francesca decided, and was interested to see how carefully Charles ignored this remark as he turned to offer his arm to Elizabeth.

"I am dashed sorry," Nigel said finally, "but you've left me behind, Miss DelSorro. Who is an idiot?"

Charles and Elizabeth exchanged comical glances, but bit back the obvious reply. Francesca was not so reticent.

"Why *you* are, Mr. Foxmoor," she said with a coquettish turn of her head. "If we are all related there must be no Miss and Mistering. I am Cousin Francesca and you are Cousin Nigel."

"And I am Cousin Emma," that young lady piped in, the first words she had been able to utter since Nigel had walked through the door, outside of an awestruck how-do-you-do.

Mrs. Locke felt quite happy as she saw them off—she did so enjoy seeing young people enjoy themselves, and was most pleased to have discovered a long-lost branch of the family.

There was barely room for all of them in the carriage, for it had been built to seat four, but the three girls squeezed into the rear with much giggling until Nigel protested, "But this will never do! You cannot leave Buckley to sit next to me and deprive us both of female company."

Francesca and Elizabeth cast each other a glance, and with instant mutual consent nominated Emma to ride in the front with Nigel, for the plain fact of the matter was that Emma took up more room than either of them and even more room than Charles. The new arrangement suited them all, and they were soon off.

Presently, Elizabeth turned to Charlie, who was comfortably situated between Francesca and her, and said, "I did not know you were acquainted with Mr. Foxmoor, but I am certainly not disappointed that you brought him along. His carriage is much nicer than yours."

"And how am I to reply to that?" he asked with a grin. "Do I thank you for the compliment about my choice of friends, or should I growl about the slight you have given my carriage and pair?"

"You should consider *that* remark a compliment, too," Elizabeth told him playfully, "for I could say much worse about your equestrian equipage."

" 'Equestrian equipage,' " he repeated with admiration. "A very nice, alliterative phrase. I shall remember it."

Elizabeth ignored him as she leaned over to whisper

31

importantly to Francesca, "Mr. Foxmoor was in love with Anna, you know!"

Something of her desired effect was lost when Francesca asked, "Who is Anna?"

"My stepmama!" Elizabeth said.

Francesca shook her head in mock consternation. "You will have to draw me a picture of our family, Elizabeth. I become more confused every minute. Will there be more cousins popping up here and there? Or perhaps we are related to everyone in London."

"If you traced the lines back far enough, you would discover that we are," Charles said seriously.

"Charlie, please don't go all scholarly on us. You are not at Oxford any longer," Elizabeth said dauntingly.

"I should not mind meeting another cousin like Nigel," Francesca decided. "He is a very fine-looking gentleman. Tell me, is he a lord?"

Elizabeth laughed and explained the reference to Charles.

"Quite the contrary," Charlie said with mock gravity. "He rather fancies himself as Shelley's monster."

"No!" Elizabeth exclaimed with all the proper astonishment. "Why does he fancy that, in heaven's name?"

"Because they both desire a wife!" He and Elizabeth laughed together gleefully.

"Shelley's monster—not another relation?" Francesca asked with some distress.

Charles and Elizabeth laughed all the harder.

"Yes, that is Charlie's real father," Elizabeth said at last. "He went quite mad and his keeper was called Shelley." She clapped her hand to her mouth. "Oh, forgive me, Charlie, I promised never to reveal that to another living soul."

"Really, Lizzie," Charlie said with a sniff, "I don't go making a show of all your darkest secrets. You might have a little respect for the dead—or at least for the mad."

Elizabeth said to Francesca gravely, "I do think you have a right to hear of it. It is an inherited failing, and sometimes, usually at the time of the full moon, Charlie himself becomes quite frightening. It is only fair to warn you beforehand."

"You are both making fun at my expense," Francesca said, "but I do not mind. Later I will ask Cousin Nigel myself who this Shelley's monster is and will find true enlightenment."

"The fun seems to be all at my expense," Charles said, "if this monster is supposed to be my father, as Lizzie said."

"Perhaps it is true, after all," Elizabeth persisted. "How are you to know—your father died when you were quite small."

"And so even my pitiful orphaned status is to be no more than the butt of a joke."

"Pooh," Elizabeth said succinctly. "Francesca, this seems to me a marvelous opportunity for you to tell us all about your native Spain, before you grow too weary of the subject."

Charles agreed that this would interest him mightily, and so Francesca addressed herself to giving a suitably detailed description and they passed a very pleasant half hour in this way. Nigel Foxmoor's driving was indeed commendable, the carriage comfortable and well sprung. Every now and then Emma's voice drifted back to them, and they heard her describing her ball gown yet again to her captive audience. All was pleasant until the sun, which had been lurking behind a cloud all the while, exposed itself and Elizabeth remembered her potential freckles and reached for her parasol. This was found with some difficulty, underneath Mr. Charles Buckley, who had been thinking that Foxmoor's carriage was not as well built as he had been led to believe.

"Really, Charlie, you are so thoughtless at times," Elizabeth said crossly when presented with the broken mess that had been her parasol.

"It wasn't my fault," Charles said mildly. "You should have moved it before I sat down."

"It was bran new," Elizabeth complained. "One would think you would have felt it poking into you, but

33

I suppose it is true that where there is no sense there is no feeling."

"If you are going to indulge in clichés, Lizzie, at least use them in their proper context," Charles said with a slight show of temper.

"I thought I was remarkably apt, myself, and don't call me Lizzie," she said petulantly. "You probably wouldn't feel a thing if you sat on a bed of nails."

"Do not indulge in gross exaggeration, either, Elizabeth. It is most unbecoming and shows a want of imagination," Charles said with an air of superiority. "As a matter of fact, I thought the fault lay with Foxmoor's carriage and was trying to be civil and not complain. Had I known it was your deuced umbrella—"

"It is a parasol, and don't swear," Elizabeth interrupted. "And I don't see why you have to bring Mr. Foxmoor into this. You are merely trying to gloss over the fact that you were at fault, and you know it."

"I was not at fault! If anyone is, you are. You can see how tightly squeezed we are back here—you should have held the damned thing on your lap!"

"Charlie! Your language!" She glanced around, hoping the pedestrians nearby had not heard him.

"Don't come the prude with me, Elizabeth. *You* taught me that word when you were a hooligan of five, and I an orphaned lad of seven."

Elizabeth was about to retort again, but suddenly realized that she sounded exactly like that five-year-old hooligan at that very moment, and so she laughed instead. "I declare, Charlie, it is almost fun to argue with you again. I had not realized how I missed it."

"It reminds me of that time you accused me of breaking your doll—and your arguments have hardly improved since then." He saw she was about to flare up again and cried, "Pax!"

Elizabeth smiled and said, "Pax." Then, to Francesca, "I must apologize for both Charles and me—we must sound like two squabbling schoolchildren to you."

"No need to apologize," Francesca said graciously.

"In fact, I find it most entertaining. *Most* entertaining." She gave a knowing smile.

The party returned to Upper Grosvenor Street for tea, and by the end of the afternoon even those who had been strangers only the day before now felt like old friends. Nigel discovered that they were all expected at the Waters' that evening, and was confident that he would see them all there. Though he had received no invitation to the event, he had been an admirer of Lady Imogen Waters when she was still Lady Imogen Westham, back in the days of his confirmed bachelorhood. Certainly she would not refuse him entrance, he told his new friends confidently as he parted from them. He lingered longest over Francesca's hand, and while she did not know who Shelley's monster was, she was more than content with the information that Mr. Foxmoor was seeking a wife.

# THREE

A musical soirée would not seem to be the kind of
entertainment that would send flutters of excitement
into a young girl's heart, especially one like Elizabeth
Durant, who was embarking on her fourth season and
had already sampled much more heady amusements,
such as masked balls and a royal wedding. In comparison, this evening would be so mild that even Emma
Locke, who was not yet out, was allowed to attend, and
while it was quite the thing to express appreciation of
the foremost soprano in London, Elizabeth herself could
never truly enjoy that kind of music. For one thing, the
songs would probably be sung in Italian, of which
Elizabeth had no knowledge, and furthermore she would
be expected to express an unfelt admiration for the
performance afterwards. It would doubtless be hot and
stuffy in Lady Imogen's drawing room and there would
be no dancing or games, but only a light supper accompanied by a great deal of idle chatter.

Why then did Elizabeth display every symptom of a
young girl about to attend her first ball? Why did she
agonize so over choosing her attire, dismissing one
gown as too fancy, another as too plain, before settling
upon an unpretentious but elegant frock of saffron
silk? Why did she display an uncharacteristic burst of
temper at her maid when, after half an hour of fid-
dling, her hair was still not exactly as she wished it to

be? Why should this particular evening appear to have all the importance of a presentation at court?

For the simple reason that Lady Imogen Waters was sister to the handsome and eligible Lord Westbridge, with whom Elizabeth had recently and irrevocably fallen in love.

That Lord Westbridge might not wish to subject himself to what promised to be a boring and educational gathering was a dreadful possibility Elizabeth did not allow herself to consider. He *must* be there. She had already rehearsed seven times how she would address him, in what subtle manner she would remind him of the pleasant dinner they had shared side by side last week, of the three dances they had enjoyed together on three different occasions, and of course, even more subtly, where he might be expected to encounter her again in the near future.

Elizabeth had never felt this way before about any of the young gentlemen of her acquaintance. She had never lacked for suitors, and had even received more than her fair share of marriage proposals, but never before had a gentleman raised more than the slightest fluttering in her breast. Since she had met Lord Westbridge three weeks before, however, all that had changed. She thought of him constantly and counted the days until she might meet him again. If he was not present at an event, the entire evening fell flat, and if he was present, Elizabeth was conscious every moment of where he stood and to whom he spoke. Most especially did she notice when he spoke to any other young lady, feeling for the first time in her life the cruel pangs of jealousy.

A week ago had come the exhilarating realization that she was indeed in love with Lord Westbridge. They had been partners at a dinner in honor of the retirement of one of England's great generals, held at the house of Lord Westbridge's father, the Duke of Duxton. Lord Westbridge had donned his old uniform for the occasion and in Elizabeth's eyes appeared more handsome and majestic than ever. They had conversed most intently during dinner, and danced together afterwards, and Elizabeth was assured by the meaningful way he had pressed her hand when the dance was over that she had made quite an impression on him. The only thing left to do now was to make sure that he fell in love with her, and Elizabeth had no doubts that this could be accomplished most speedily.

Elizabeth would have been gratified indeed had she known that the object of her affection was at that very moment on his way to his sister's house and had actually been wondering whether he would see Elizabeth there tonight. Not so gratifying would be the names of the other four ladies about whom he wondered the same thing, but perhaps even this information would have been made tolerable by the knowledge that Lord Westbridge, like Mr. Foxmoor, had embarked upon this season with a steadfast determination to find himself a wife.

Ivor, Lord Westbridge felt he was already making progress in this direction. The season was only a few weeks old and already he had a mental list of some dozen young ladies of good family, some with fortunes, some with beauty, and some, like Elizabeth Durant, with a little of both to recommend them. He would subtract from or add to this list as he saw fit in the next several months. For instance, someone would be deleted should she show an unfortunate tendency to cackle instead of laugh, or if he discovered that her fortune was insufficient to make up for her lack of beauty. And then there were any number of young ladies he had not even met yet who might prove eligible. He had decided that halfway through the season, if one of these ladies did not clearly outshine her rivals, he would actually write the list down with appropriate columns for scoring them on the basis of beauty, fortune, intelligence, et cetera, and make his decision from that information.

So why should a gentleman with no more serious pursuits to occupy his time than to pick and choose among London's prettiest maidens, any one of whom would be more than happy to wed him, approach his task with such a look of grim determination on his face? For the simple reason that it was not Lord Westbridge's desire that he should marry, but his obligation. He would have been content to go through life a bachelor, in fact would have preferred it. He found an evening spent at his club, talking over old campaigns with some good brandy to wash the hyperboles down, infinitely more enjoyable than a night of stultifying boredom at Almack's asking simpering misses to stand up with him. Much did he prefer an evening's visit to the pleasant little house in Soho wherein resided a certain Mistress Santini, one of the spoils of his victories in Spain, to an evening of dancing with ingenuous schoolgirls who trod on his toes and fluttered their eyelashes at him. His life had been ordered quite to his liking since his return from the wars three years before, and little did he savor the necessity of making a change.

But the cruel fact remained that Lord Westbridge was heir to a dukedom, and as such must insure the succession by finding himslf a duchess.

To the casual observer, unacquainted with all the facts about his family, this object might seem unnecessary, for his father had a young wife who had already presented him with two healthy sons and was increasing yet again. But between Ivor and his young half-brother Lord Jasper stood yet another brother, whose name, if it was mentioned at all, was mentioned in whispers—and never to the duke himself. For Lord Ingram was the blot on the family copy book, the legendary black sheep of the family. He had fled the country in disgrace some eight years previous, a traitor to the crown. It was only through his continued correspondence with Lady Imogen that the family had learned he had actually married a West Indian woman and was well on his way to rearing a large passel of half-bred brats. That the succession should pass to this scapegrace through any failure on Lord Westbridge's part to secure the succession where it belonged was not to be thought of.

Thus the comfortable life he had lived since Napoleon had been sent into exile for the second, and one hoped last, time was now over for Ivor. He had a mission in life, a duty he saw just as clearly as his father did, when the duke had pointed out to his son that it was time he looked to his and the family's future. Ivor must find a wife, and he would not find her idling at his club or in a little house in Soho. He was three and thirty; in a very few years he would be even more set in his ways and the contemplation of matrimony would be even more distasteful to him. The thing must be done and done expediently, and if that required attendance at musical evenings and Almack's every Wednesday night, not to mention the innumerable balls, concerts, theater parties, visits to the opera, and probably even outings to Richmond when the weather became warmer, then Lord Westbridge would grit his teeth and bear it with honor, as became a Westham. After all, he had licked the French; he could certainly prove himself equal to this present challenge.

"So you have come, Ivor," Lady Imogen said unenthusiastically when her brother strolled into her drawing room, where she was putting the finishing touches on the flowers she had arranged to decorate the room. "You are rather early."

Lord Westbridge gave his sister a peck on the cheek, which embrace missed its mark somewhat and landed in midair. "I was never one to shirk my duty—you know that, Imogen."

"Yes, I do," she said, giving him a fleeting smile. "You must excuse me; I have to make sure that Percy is ready." She floated out of the room, leaving a trail of rich, exotic scent behind her that Lord Westbridge sniffed appreciatively.

He sighed and sat himself down in one of the chairs that had been arranged for the audience. If only he could find a woman like Imogen, he thought, he would be well suited. His sister was tall and dark, with

40

flashing black eyes and an elegant figure that she clothed in raiment sure to catch a gentleman's eye, which gaze she returned boldly. The years he had spent on the Peninsula had taught Ivor a preference for dark women with no nonsense about them. To return to the social scene in London had been more than distasteful to him, it had been perplexing, for he knew not how to deal with these pale, fluttering misses who all seemed to think it was alluring to keep their heads down and look up at him through their eyelashes. To his mind, it showed rather too much of the whites of their eyes to be attractive. You would never see Imogen look at a fellow in that way. Straight into the eyes, that was Lady Imogen's style, and that was what Ivor liked.

He gave a rueful little shake of his head as he wondered again how Imogen had done no better for herself than Percy Waters. Of course, all that business had happened while he was out of the country. He could not help feeling that if he had been there to put his foot down things might have turned out quite differently. He would have seen that Ingram had been held on a tighter rein and married to a suitable Englishwoman of fortune. Imogen, too, would have made a much better marriage if Ivor had been there to supervise. Then he could have been left to live his life as he chose, satisfied that the succession would pass to Ingram's legitimate, English offspring, instead of displaying himself night after night in the "Marriage Mart," the sole purpose of his life to treat every social engagement like an auction at Tattersoll's.

Lady Imogen swept back into the room, leading her husband like an obedient puppy dog. Percy Waters was a pleasant enough chap, and his doting admiration for his wife was still quite obvious even after five years of marriage. Ivor could almost forgive him his overfondness for drink.

Lord Westbridge stood up to shake his hand, and Percy greeted him in his usual jolly manner. They exchanged a few pleasantries, but Ivor was distressed by the reek of gin about him. Really, if Percy had to drink, couldn't he at least choose something with a bit more style? It did not reflect well on the family. As soon as his own future was settled, Ivor would see if he could not do something about his brother-in-law.

It was not long before the other guests began arriving and Ivor was put through the excruciating torment of remembering the names of young ladies he had met only twice or thrice previously. When Elizabeth Durant came up to him he was quite relieved, for hers was a name he remembered with no trouble—Elizabeth had impressed him as another straight-in-the-eyes young woman. But who in the world was this fluttering little pale thing she was towing along with her?

"My lord, I don't believe you have met my cousin, Emma Locke," Elizabeth said. "Emma, the Marquess of Westbridge."

Emma extended her hand limply and gazed up at Ivor through sparse eyelashes. "Indeed, I have seen *you* about, my lord, although I am certain you have not noticed *me*." She giggled.

Lord Westbridge was not so rude as to mention that he certainly had not.

"And this is another cousin of mine, Francesca DelSorro," Elizabeth said, now introducing him to someone who was the exact antithesis of the first cousin he had met. If he had not been so astonished by Miss DelSorro's resemblance to his sister, he might have wondered how one family could produce such widely divergent types.

"How do you do," Miss DelSorro said, and Ivor detected the trace of an accent.

"Miss Durant appears to have a far-reaching family," Lord Westbridge said. "You are not English, I take it."

"Indeed not—I am from Spain," she replied without hesitation. "But, my lord, we have met already—do you not remember me?"

Lord Westbridge shook his head apologetically. "I am afraid I have a terrible memory for names and faces."

Francesca laughed. "I should be crushed by disappointment, my lord, but I do not blame you. When last you saw me I was no more than a schoolgirl. You occupied me in Spain—do you recall now?"

"Occupied you?" Lord Westbridge inquired with raised eyebrows. He had "occupied" a great many women in Spain, but certainly never a schoolgirl.

"With your army!" Francesca persisted. "You were stationed in my father's house in Madrid, do you not recall?"

"Of course!" Lord Westbridge said with relief, glad to know that she was using "occupied" in its proper military sense and did not mean anything else by it. "Don Pedro DelSorro was your father, and a very lovely house it was, too. And what brings you to England, Miss DelSorro—or should I call you Doña Francesca as I used to?"

"Ah! You do remember me. I am most relieved." She smiled. "I am come to England because my Spanish lover was most unsuitable and I hope to find myself an English husband," she explained simply.

Lord Westbridge tried to hide a smile, and Emma Locke gasped and turned beet-red.

"Have I said something I oughtn't?" Francesca asked ingenuously.

Elizabeth laughed lightly. "You must excuse my cousin, my lord; as you have surmised, she is new to our shores."

"Not at all," he said gallantly. "I find such candor quite refreshing, and she is quite right, too. No one makes a more suitable husband than an Englishman." He graced Miss DelSorro with another smile, to prove to her he had not taken offense, and addressed a few words to her in Spanish, asking after her father and some of the other gentlemen he had known there. After they had exchanged a few more remarks in that language, Ivor excused himself, as he noticed another family arriving to whom he must pay his courtesies.

"Oh, Francesca, *really*, that was very terrible of you," Emma said as soon as he had left them.

"It was nothing more than the truth," Francesca

43

pointed out, not in the least contrite. "I should not tell people why I am here, then?"

"Perhaps it would be better if you just explained that you are on a visit," Elizabeth suggested. "It tends to put men off if they know you are actively seeking a husband."

"But are we not all actively seeking husbands—just as they are actively seeking wives?"

"Of course, but we do not *speak* of it," Elizabeth told her.

"I see," Francesca said. "Then you do not wish for me to tell my lord, the marquess, that you have set your cap at him?"

"Certainly not!" Elizabeth exclaimed, turning almost as red as Emma had.

"Very well," Francesca said. "I will comply, although it seems to me that things would progress much faster for you if you came right out and declared your intentions. But then I keep forgetting that you are English and prefer the subtlety."

"Indeed I do," Elizabeth avowed.

"Nonetheless, I think my old friendship with Lord Westbridge can be used to your advantage," Francesca said happily, but when Elizabeth was about to protest again, she assured her hastily, "Do not fret, Elizabeth. If it is your desire to let him think that he is pursuing you and not otherwise, I will do nothing to alter that supposition in him. It is somewhat the same in Spain— men always like to be the hunters and not the hunted, do they not?"

"Yes," Elizabeth agreed with a sigh, "and it does make things difficult at times."

"Never mind," Francesca told her. "I have decided that Lord Westbridge is most suitable for you and I will do anything I can to help you bring him to the mark."

"Thank you, Francesca," Elizabeth said with some reservation. "But you needn't be *quite* so colloquial in your English, you know."

"That is good." She nodded thoughtfully. "You tell me of these things and I will learn to comply. Now here are your cousin Charles and his very beautiful friend. How pleasant—I think I will go set my cap at Mr. Foxmoor. He will fit in most nicely with my plans." And without further ado, she approached the two young men, Elizabeth trailing in her wake, shaking her head and wondering exactly what plans Francesca had in mind.

The performance that followed was fully as boring as Elizabeth had anticipated, but her attention was occupied elsewhere. Before they found seats, Lord Westbridge had engaged her for supper afterwards, so she heard barely a note as she went over in her mind just what she would say to him and how she could advance one step further toward securing his love.

Unfortunately, she found no opportunity to use any of her rehearsed speeches, for at the supper table Emma, who joined them with her partner of the evening, Charles Buckley, dominated the conversation. She could not praise the soprano highly enough and even admitted, with a modest blush, that she did some singing herself. Elizabeth groaned inwardly, hoping fervently that there would be no opportunity for Emma to display her dubious talents that evening.

"But did you not find her vibrato rather uneven?" Francesca asked Emma earnestly.

Emma regarded her blankly.

"I am sorry, I thought the word was the same in English," Francesca said. "Lord Westbridge, perhaps you could translate."

"No, you are quite right, cousin," Charles put in. "It was the correct word and a very apt comment, too. I agree with you completely."

"Yes, and her diction was rather—now I do not know the word." Francesca laughed. "One had difficulty understanding her."

"I should say so!" Nigel Foxmoor exclaimed. "She wasn't even singing in English."

"Perhaps the word you seek is sloppy," Charles suggested, "but as I know little Italian myself I could not say whether I agree with you or not on that score."

"Her diction was definitely sloppy," Francesca decided. "Although that may have been partly the fault of the hall. One cannot obtain the proper resonance when singing at full voice in a small room, as she did."

"You obviously know a great deal about the subject," Charles said.

"I have studied it a little," Francesca admitted.

"My interest in opera is only of very recent origin," Charles said. "A friend of mine, Richard Tanner, introduced me to Rossini and Paisiello only recently. Of course, I do not sing myself, but I do play upon the pianoforte."

"That is an accomplishment I have never been able to master," Francesca said regretfully.

They went on to discuss the strengths and failings of various composers, and Francesca described the difficulties of singing in German as opposed to Italian. Lord Westbridge felt rather disgruntled that his ignorance in things musical did not allow him to shine in this particular conversation, and that the only opinion he could offer was that he found Mr. Buckley nearly as dull as the singer, a comment civility prevented him from expressing. Then Elizabeth smiled at him and said she did so hate people who showed off their superior knowledge and wasn't it nicer to know nothing at all about opera and so be able to declare without reservation that one had witnessed a great performance?

Ivor laughed and smiled warmly, placing Miss Durant a few notches higher on his mental list.

Emma and Nigel, equally ignorant of music, were content to discuss the diva's gown, which had been most striking, and Emma was most truly grateful when Mr. Foxmoor assured her earnestly that he could easily picture Emma herself in such a gown. She even went so far as to think it was almost a shame that she was as good as promised to Charles, for she found Mr. Foxmoor a compatible companion, even though his eyes kept wandering to Francesca, who was most elegant tonight in a gown of orange satin.

To his surprise, Lord Westbridge almost enjoyed

himself that evening. Elizabeth Durant was adept at making interesting small talk, and he gave her some bonus points on his mental balance sheet, for such a facility was indispensable in the wife of one who hoped to hold an important governmental post one day. However, he was not ready to commit himself yet, and generously added Miss DelSorro to his list, her most obvious assets being their old acquaintance and her fortunate resemblance to his sister.

# FOUR

The next evening Francesca DelSorro attended her
first London ball and it was plain to all that she
was destined to make a great splash that season. The
gentlemen seemed to flock around her, queuing up for
an introduction, for to them she had the double attrac-
tions of novelty and a sophistication rarely seen in her
English counterparts. If she were not already in love
with Lord Westbridge, Elizabeth might have been jealous of her cousin, for many of Francesca's conquests
had been equally devoted to Elizabeth herself only the
year before.

Dutifully, Francesca sought her uncle's permission
when invitations from her numerous suitors began
pouring in, and rare was the day she was not engaged
to drive out in the park with one gentleman after
receiving morning calls from at least three others.
Nigel Foxmoor soon became her most persistent admirer, for he was quite taken with this dark-eyed beauty
straight out of one of his Gothic romances, and each
time he came to call he had memorized yet another
pertinent passage from one of these volumes designed
to win Francesca's heart.

After only a week she received her first proposal of
marriage, from Henry Simpson, a goggle-eyed youth
with a penchant for poetry, which he presented to his
beloved in the form of parchment scrolls, done up with

48

much red sealing wax and tied with a ribbon. Francesca related his stuttering proposal to Elizabeth the day after it had taken place when their morning visitors had left them alone and the two girls finally had a moment to exchange confidences.

"Why, those are almost the exact words he used to me!" Elizabeth responded gleefully.

"I am crushed!" Francesca exclaimed. "He told me most distinctly that he had never loved any woman as he loved me."

"I am so sorry to disappoint you, dear Francesca," Elizabeth said with mock gravity, "but it was not quite a year ago that he whispered the very same thing to *me*." She sighed. "I remember it quite well. 'Elizabeth,' he said, 'I l-l-l-love you.' "

They both dissolved into fits of merriment at the expense of this poor unfortunate who apparently proposed to any lady who took the trouble of hearing him through.

"It seems to me that you progress with Lord Westbridge," Francesca remarked, after the subject of Henry Simpson had been thoroughly explored for all its possible humor.

Elizabeth sighed. "I wish I could agree with you," she said, "but it does not seem to me that he treats me with any greater particularity than anyone else."

"That is not so," Francesca protested. "Did you not stand up with him two times last night?"

"Yes, but so did you, and so did Mary Bridges and several other young ladies."

"Not so," Francesca argued. "I watched him most carefully, and you and I were the only ones to dance with him twice. And when I danced with him, we spoke only of you."

"Truly?" Elizabeth asked eagerly. "What did he say about me?"

"Let me see," Francesca said with a great show of concentration. "I said something to the effect that I admired your coloring and complexion and then he said that he liked dark girls just as well."

"But that was a compliment to you, not to me," Elizabeth pointed out, disappointed.

"Exactly, and so I told him, but then I asked him if he did not think you were the embodiment of what an English beauty should be—no, no, do not be embarrassed, Elizabeth, for he agreed wholeheartedly, let me assure you. Then I asked him if he had any particular fondness for you."

"Francesca!" Elizabeth cried, horrified. "How could you be so bold? I am quite certain you have spoiled my chances completely."

"Certainly not. Do not think that I came out and said it in so many words—although if he were Spanish I might have. But in the one week I have been here I have already learned much of English subtlety. I merely remarked that I had grown very fond of you and admired you greatly, and did he not think it was right of me to do so. He agreed most enthusiastically.

"Of course he did," Elizabeth said glumly. "Out of civility he was forced to do so, but how does that indicate that he shares your fondness for me?"

"Because he said so." She took a pause as she strove to remember his exact words. "He said, 'Miss Durant is a very attractive young lady and I cannot help but agree with you. I confess to sharing your feeling for her.' Those were his very words."

Elizabeth jumped up. "Oh, Francesca, did he really say that? Then he does care for me a little, do you think?"

"Did I not just tell you so? Then I hinted, in the most *subtle* way, that perhaps his feelings for you were reciprocated."

Elizabeth's expression of rapture changed to one of consternation. "Oh, no, Francesca, he will think me most dreadfully forward."

"How can he think that when it was *I* who told him? Especially when I insisted that you were far too well-bred ever to mention such a thing yourself. But even so, I think you *should* be a little more forward with him. Then things might progress more speedily for you. For all his great age and apparent worldliness, Lord Westbridge strikes me as one who is rather thickheaded where women are concerned."

Elizabeth did not object to this slight against her loved one, for Lord Westbridge's continuing reserve had caused her to reluctantly draw a similar conclusion. "I have tried to indicate that my interest in him is much deeper than mere flirtation," she said, "but I am afraid of putting him off completely. Whenever I speak more seriously with him, he cuts the conversation short and introduces me to someone else. Do you recall how abruptly he left our box the other evening when we were at the theater? He *said* it was because he had just seen his sister and wished to speak to her, but I know it was because he overheard Aunt Annabel remark to Uncle George what a charming picture the two of us made. And later I saw him talking not to his sister, but to that dreadful Leona Herbert. It is almost as if he is *afraid* of being too attentive to me."

"Then you are doing better than I had thought," Francesca said with satisfaction. "My dear Elizabeth, have you not learned that when a man appears most afraid of you is when his interest is the strongest?"

"No," Elizabeth said shortly. "All I know is that he has mentioned several times that he would like to take me for a drive, but has never made a definite engagement. And yesterday, when I was out shopping with Aunt Annabel and Emma, I saw him drive by with Winifred Middleton."

"Is she not that red-haired girl with the face like a horse?" Francesca inquired.

"Yes, and eight thousand a year, I am told," Elizabeth said dismally. "How am I to compete with that?"

"By using your ingenuity," Francesca said. "Elizabeth, I will not try to advise you, for you must act as you think best, but if I were in your situation I would not hesitate to use all the feminine tricks at my disposal. It is apparent that Lord Westbridge is simply unable to make up his mind, so you must help him do so. But I will say no more on the subject. I still believe you are progressing well, while I, unfortunately, am no closer to my goal."

"What do you mean? Nigel Foxmoor is practically eating out of your hand."

"Mr. Foxmoor is not a lord," Francesca said.

"True, but lords are not all that plentiful, and I doubt you would find one as beautiful as Mr. Foxmoor. Aunt Annabel tells me that he has quite a respectable fortune, too, and has inherited his grandfather's estate in Devon."

"Yes, there is everything to recommend Mr. Foxmoor, except sense. He chatters on until he gives me the headache, and then when he can think of nothing original to say, he quotes at me." She shook her head. "No, Mr. Foxmoor is not for me, but I think he and Emma would suit admirably."

Elizabeth gave a hoot of laughter. "What an amusing idea! Somehow I cannot picture them together—he is so much prettier than Emma."

"That is quite true, but I believe they would deal together admirably just the same. Elizabeth, tell me, what exactly does 'dashed' mean?"

"Dashed?"

"Mr. Foxmoor always thinks I look *dashed* beautiful and I am always wearing a *dashed* pretty gown and he is always *dashed* glad to see me."

"It is just a figure of speech," Elizabeth explained. "It means the same as very, only more so."

"Then I find Mr. Foxmoor *dashed* boring, which would make him perfect for Emma, who is also dashed boring." She gave a decided nod of her head, as if the matter were quite settled.

"I am afraid that however well you think they might be suited, Mr. Foxmoor will have to look elsewhere, for Emma is to marry Charlie," Elizabeth said. "It is almost a certainty that he will offer for her tomorrow night at her ball."

"Do you think so?" Francesca asked. "I have not noticed what you might call a particular fondness between them."

"That is only because they have known each other too long. I suppose you have not noticed a fondness between Charlie and *me* either, yet I am fond of him, in a way—he is rather like a brother to me."

"No, I would not agree with you," Francesca said. "I have noticed much more of a fondness between you and Charlie than between Emma and Charlie."

Elizabeth shook her head with amusement. "Sometimes I wonder at your powers of observation, Francesca. Of course Charlie will offer for Emma—she is counting on it."

"Yes, that I *have* noticed, so you see my powers of observation are not impaired in the least. Let us hope he does not disappoint her. I have learned that Emma crossed is not a pleasant thing."

Elizabeth certainly agreed with her there, for this past week there had been ample opportunity to observe Emma being crossed. The girl was very nervous about her debut ball and was eager to see that everything would be done correctly and as a result was frequently out of temper. In vain did her mother tell her time and again that all would be well and she had nothing to worry about; still Emma fretted and fussed. Had all the flowers been ordered and would they arrive on time? And when they did arrive, who was to arrange them? Was her Mama quite certain that the musicians were the finest available? She did not wish her ball spoiled because the music was not everything it should be.

But the thing that caused Emma most anguish was her much discussed gown. At her last fitting she had discovered that the gown was too tight—she had been indulging in too many creampuffs, the seamstress clucked to herself, though she did not tell her client this. Instead she suggested to Emma that a diet of tea and toast might be beneficial for a few days; everyone said it was so healthful and purging to the system. Emma tried this diet for one morning, but it depressed her so that she ate twice as much as usual for dinner and Mrs. Locke told the seamstress in confidence that she simply must let the dress out, which she did.

Then there was the matter of refreshments to be served. Emma did not wish lobster patties included on the menu, as they gave her a rash, and she would die of mortification should she break out in a rash at her ball. Mrs. Locke suggested, quite sensibly, that not everyone had a rash from lobster patties and they would be expected and Emma would not be forced to eat them herself.

"But I *like* them!" Emma had wailed. "And if I see them about I know I shall just be dying to have one."

So lobster patties were struck from the menu and salmon rolls substituted.

Then there was Emma's hair. Every evening the hairdresser came to try out a new style on her, so that by the time the ball came around she would have chosen the one that suited her best. But Emma cared for none of them, and a quick succession of hairdressers pleased her no better.

Indeed, it was only the certain knowledge that Charlie would offer for her that night that kept her spirits up at all, though Mrs. Locke quietly tried to discourage this expectation, for fear her daughter would be disappointed. But Emma was not to be dissuaded and her confidence in the matter was all that sustained her. When Elizabeth pointed out that if she took a second helping of dessert she would have to wear a tent instead of a gown, Emma was able to retort that in three seasons Elizabeth's trim figure had not won her a husband, whereas Emma would be betrothed the very night of her coming out. When she overheard Elizabeth and Francesca discussing how they could make certain Lord Westbridge would lead Elizabeth out for the first dance, Emma sniggered and said, "I am glad I do not have to resort to subterfuge to get a partner," for she already had Charlie's promise to perform the same office for her. Little did it matter to her that he was an indifferent dancer; after they were married they need never dance together again.

Her ill humor increased as the day of the ball approached, and she had all the household walking on eggs for fear that she would fly into a rage and cry, and then be even more angry in case her eyes remained puffy and red until the important moment. Her nervous temper extended even to Charles himself when he came to call the afternoon of the ball.

He was shown into the drawing room, where Mrs. Locke was supervising the flower arrangement.

"Aunt Annabel," he said, "I know this is a bad time to call, but I merely stopped by to see if I could make myself useful in any way."

"Dear boy," Mrs. Locke said. "So thoughtful of you. Let me call the girls; perhaps they would like you to join them for tea."

"Oh, there is no need for that if they are resting for tonight. As I said, I merely stopped by to see if I could be of any use."

"Francesca is out with that charming Mr. Foxmoor," Mrs. Locke said, "but I am sure Emma will be most pleased to see you. The poor girl is so worried that everything should go well tonight that I think a friendly visit with you will be just the thing to soothe her spirits."

She left Charles alone while she sent for her daughter, and a few minutes later Emma came in, looking rather pale and put-upon.

"What did *you* come for, Charlie?" she asked sullenly. She was not in the best of spirits, having just discovered that it was because her gown had been let out and not as a result of her single morning of tea and toast that it fitted her. "We are very busy here, as you must know."

"Yes, I do know, but I thought you might like a chance to get away for an hour or so. We could go for a drive; it is a lovely day."

"I don't see how you can be so insensitive, Charlie," Emma pouted. "I am *needed* here, and if you can't see that, then you are a greater fool than ever I thought."

Charlie continued valiantly, "Then perhaps you might have some small commission for me. Perhaps some-

55

thing you have forgotten that I might fetch from the shops for you."

"Don't be silly—what would you know about that kind of thing?" Emma slumped unceremoniously into a chair and with a desultory wave of her arm invited Charles to do the same. "Well, now you are here, I suppose you want some tea."

"No, thank you, I have just had luncheon."

"Well, *I* want some tea," Emma said, and rang the bell.

"Perhaps I should leave," Charles suggested, after some minutes had passed in silence.

"I don't mind. I cannot imagine why you came here in the first place. It was most thoughtless."

Charles Buckley was normally a very even-tempered gentleman, but even with the allowances he was making for Emma's state of mind this afternoon, he felt he would lose his temper quite soon if he was not treated with a greater degree of civility.

Fortunately, he was saved from this when Elizabeth entered to fetch a book she had left there and exclaimed quite genuinely, "Why, Charlie, I didn't know you were here. What a pleasant surprise." He smiled at her warmly and took her offered hands briefly.

"Oh, of course it is, for *you!*" Emma exclaimed, jumping up. "*You* have been out for years, for all the good it has done you. What do *you* care if my ball is a success or not? I should tell everyone what a cruel, heartless person you are and then you will never be married and won't I laugh then!" With that she burst into tears and fled from the room.

"There she goes again." Elizabeth sighed.

"It is my fault, I should not have come—I did not mean to upset her," Charles apologized.

"Nonsense," Elizabeth told him. "It has nothing to do with you; she has been insufferable all week. Now tell me, is that your carriage standing outside, with the horses looking as though they could do with a nice trot?"

"Yes, indeed," Charlie said.

"Do you think they would mind trotting down to the shops where I could choose some new ribbons? I have just discovered that the ribbons on the gown I am to wear tonight are soiled and I am in desperate need of some new ones."

"I am sure they—and I—would be delighted. In fact, I just offered to perform the same service for Emma, with the results you have already seen."

"Then I am sorry you have to take second best," Elizabeth said. "I shan't be a moment."

"You are never second best to me, Lizzie," Charlie said, but she was already out the door to collect her things and did not hear him.

"Charlie," she asked later in a subdued voice as Charles drove her to the draper's, "do you think there is any truth in what Emma says?"

"What exactly does she say?" Charlie had long ago stopped listening to Emma when she was in a temper.

"Do you think there is something wrong with me? After all, it is my fourth season and I am not yet married. I am already twenty years old." This last was in anguished tones.

Charlie hid his amusement politely, realizing that his cousin was quite seriously worried and would not appreciate merely a light reassurance that she was far from being put on the shelf. "You have received some offers of marriage, have you not?" he asked.

"Yes, but they do not count," Elizabeth said.

"Do you mean the gentlemen in question were not sincere?"

"I suppose they were, but I did not love any of them."

"Then I think that far from there being something wrong with you, you have shown great good sense in not entering a marriage where you would not have been happy."

"But I have not received one proposal yet this year!" Elizabeth pointed out. "Does that not indicate that it is generally accepted that I *am* on the shelf, despite what you say?"

Charlie could not keep from laughing this time, and Elizabeth was injured.

"I am happy you find me so amusing. Next I will discover that I am generally referred to as a *tonic*, and you can really split your sides then."

"I doubt that sincerely," Charlie said. "Elizabeth, normally I would not discuss such things with a lady, but since you seem so low I will tell you anyway. Your name is a most active one at White's."

"What is that supposed to mean?" Elizabeth asked suspiciously.

"Surely you have heard that it is quite common to bet on the possibilities of matches. Your name is on the books in connection with several gentlemen."

"I am not sure that is at all proper," Elizabeth said primly, but she was pleased nonetheless. After a brief pause, she ventured timidly, "And whom do the odds favor, Charlie?"

He glanced at her briefly. "If you must know, the money is riding on Westbridge."

"On Westbridge! How amusing!" She attempted to be casual, but could not hide her joy at this disclosure, nor did she notice that Charlie's spirits lowered even as hers rose. She squeezed his arm in a friendly manner. "Thank you for telling me that, Charlie. We may have our falling-outs from time to time, but you always know how to cheer me up in the end. You are a true friend."

"And I hope I may always be," Charlie murmured, but there was a small measure of irony in his voice.

With the application of witch hazel to her eyes and the ingestion of a comforting cordial, Emma was soon restored to spirits by her mother. Her dress finally fit her perfectly, and even her hair was dressed to her satisfaction. When she danced the first dance with Charles she was almost radiant, for he complimented her very prettily and accepted her apology for her earlier behavior most graciously. She anticipated with a happy tingle the moment he would draw her aside to ask her hand in marriage.

Elizabeth was much cheered by her talk with Charlie. She had been thinking hard of the advice Francesca had given her, too. All Westbridge needed was some gentle prodding in the right direction, and Elizabeth thought she knew how this might be done. What she had in mind had worked once before, when she had done it just for practice and refused the subsequent marriage proposal. By the time she was dressed for the ball and had viewed her reflection with immense satisfaction, she felt a heartening and renewed confidence in her own abilities. She even rehearsed in her mind how modestly and tenderly she would make the announcement of her own betrothal after Emma had made hers.

From the beginning her plans went well. It was the easiest thing in the world to make sure Lord Westbridge was her partner for the first dance, and somehow she managed to make all the remarks she had practiced beforehand and produce exactly the right replies. Even when she danced the next few sets with other gentlemen, she was aware of Lord Westbridge's eyes upon her frequently and knew that she had made quite an impression.

She was engaged to dance with Westbridge one more time before supper and once again had planned exactly what she would say when he approached her.

"My lord, my feet are nearly worn out," she told him, smiling most brilliantly. "Do you mind if we go somewhere quiet and sit this one out together?"

"Not at all," he agreed readily. Lord Westbridge was not without his vanity and thus had been flattered in a most delightful way when he had learned from Miss DelSorro of Miss Durant's interest in him, which had been confirmed most charmingly by the young lady herself by her behavior tonight. Besides that, Miss Durant was already high on his list; she deserved this opportunity to demonstrate to him whether she should be placed at the top.

Elizabeth led him to her uncle's study, where she knew they would be undisturbed.

"It was becoming frightfully hot in there," she said as she closed the door behind them, "but I am afraid it is rather too cool to walk out in the garden, although I notice some hardy souls are doing so." She pulled the draperies shut as she said this, for the window overlooked the back garden and she did not wish to be spied upon from any quarter.

"Quite an impressive collection of books," Lord Westbridge commented. He was at a loss for what else he might say, for despite his bravado and list-making, he seldom knew what to speak of to a young lady of quality. He was grateful that Miss Durant was not at a similar loss.

"Do you do much reading, my lord?" she asked.

"Oh, yes; of course, history is my favorite. I just finished reading Proudfoot's account of the Battle of Waterloo. I found it excellent."

"Yes, of course," Elizabeth murmured, wondering how they could get off this topic and on to one of a more personal nature. She gazed up at Lord Westbridge through her eyelashes invitingly, unaware of how much this distracted him.

"Have you quite recovered from the heat yet, Miss Durant?" he asked presently. "I think there is still time to join our set, if you wish to."

"I believe I would rather remain here for a little while longer, my lord," Elizabeth said.

"Whatever you like," he replied, and went back to examining the bookshelves. He wondered if he had been too hasty in adding those extra points to Miss Durant's score.

Elizabeth felt a small degree of impatience with him. He seemed completely unaware that they were in a closed room together and completely uninformed as to what his next move should be. She decided to enact the major part of her plan and hasten things along.

"Oh!" she exclaimed suddenly.

Lord Westbridge turned to her. "What is the matter?"

"I believe I have something in my eye," she said. "This room is so dusty. I am afraid my uncle does not take proper care of his collection."

"Here, you mustn't rub it like that, it will only make things worse," Lord Westbridge admonished, taking out a large pocket handkerchief. "Let me be of assistance." He bent over her and examined the eye carefully. "I do not see anything. Perhaps it has been washed away already."

Now Lord Westbridge was not completely inexperienced where women were concerned, it was just that his experience with young English ladies was rather limited. However, he thought he could pretty much guess when any woman, whatever nationality or social status she might enjoy, was just aching to be kissed, and as Miss Durant had her face turned up to his in a most engaging manner, and as she did have quite an inviting pair of lips, he felt he might be less than a gentleman were he not to oblige.

Elizabeth should have felt quite satisfied that her little ruse had worked so well, and indeed she would have been had Lord Westbridge's kiss been a little more passionate, and a little less stiff and dutiful. Truth to tell, it was not her first experience of being kissed and she knew it could be done more expertly. But this was a beginning, and surely Ivor held better kisses in reserve.

The embrace was brief, and as soon as it was finished Lord Westbridge was all apologies. "Miss Durant! I am so sorry! I don't know what came over me! You must excuse the liberty; I promise you it will not happen again."

Elizabeth wanted no such promise, but she reassured him, feeling certain that if he would only calm down he would realize that he could now do nothing less than propose to her.

But Lord Westbridge, upon realizing the same, did a foolish thing—he panicked. He was not yet ready for

61

this step, he had not yet weighed all the possibilities, it was too early in the season, and he did not like being *pushed,* which was undoubtedly what Miss Durant had done. He apologized again and again, and then did the only thing he thought possible. He left the room, closing the door firmly behind him.

# FIVE

Charles Buckley could not find his partner for the next dance. He thought it rather odd, for she had been in plain sight until about ten minutes before; then he remembered seeing her speak to Lord Westbridge and take him aside. Well, there was Westbridge now; Charlie would simply ask him what had become of Elizabeth.

"Excuse me, my lord, but I seem to have mislaid Miss Durant," he said. "We are engaged for the next dance."

"Engaged?" Lord Westbridge repeated, a vague look in his eyes.

"I thought you might know where she is," Charlie persisted.

"Where she is? Miss Durant?" Lord Westbridge took a deep breath and gathered his thoughts. "Yes, I—er—left her in the library. I expect you can still find her there."

"Thank you," Charlie said, and if he had known Westbridge just a little better, he might have warned him against imbibing too much punch.

Elizabeth was indeed still in the library, and Charlie discovered her in a state of some disarray, mopping up what appeared to be very recent tears.

"Lizzie?" he said hesitantly, pausing at the door.

"Oh, Charlie!" Elizabeth wailed, and to his surprise she flung herself into his arms. Fortunately, he had had the foresight to close the door behind him as soon as he noticed his cousin's distress and so there were no witnesses to the touching scene where Elizabeth sobbed against his shoulder as he stroked her hair gently, murmuring, "There, there."

"Oh, Charlie, my life is ruined!" she declared when her sobs had subsided somewhat.

"Now, now, of course it is not. How could your life be ruined?" He was reluctant to release her, but thought it best not to press his advantage.

"What do you know of it? It *is* ruined. I have made a complete and utter fool of myself." She ended with a wail and again took refuge on Charlie's sturdy shoulder. Even as he searched his mind for words to soothe her, he reflected what a pleasant occupation comforting his cousin was, something he had not had the opportunity to practice for quite ten years, although he considered that he was doing it rather well for all his lack of recent practice. Of course, it would have been even more pleasant to hold her thus were she not sobbing so pitifully and doubtless making a complete mess of his coat; but that was but a small price to pay.

Presently, she quieted again and Charles led her over to the small leather divan and sat her down upon it, handing her his pocket handkerchief as he took a place next to her.

"Thank you," she mumbled, tucking away the tiny square of lace she had been using and drying her eyes with Charlie's much more serviceable piece of linen.

"Now then," Charles said, once this operation had been completed. "Would you care to tell me what is troubling you? I cannot think it can be so terrible as to ruin your life."

"You don't know the half of it," she said, smoothing the handkerchief out and folding it into squares of ever-decreasing size. "I have been an utter and complete fool! I practically threw myself at Lord Westbridge—and he didn't catch me!" She appeared ready to launch into fresh wailing until she noticed a small smile playing on Charlie's lips. "I suppose you find it all very amusing!" she declared indignantly.

"Not at all, not at all," he assured her hastily. "I was merely admiring the neatness of your metaphor."

"Although I do not see why you shouldn't laugh," she said, unfolding the handkerchief and refolding it into triangles. "I will probably be the laughingstock of London by tomorrow morning, so there is no reason you shouldn't be the first to enjoy the joke. I expect it will make a very amusing story at his club, and soon it will be known all over that I am *fast* and no one will every marry me. My life is ruined."

Charlie disagreed again, and they wasted several minutes in a yes-it-is, no-it-isn't argument until he laid one hand firmly upon her shoulder, looked her straight in the eyes, and said:

"First of all, Westbridge is a gentleman and has too much honor to tell such a tale anywhere. Aside from the fact that no gentleman would bandy a lady's name about lightly, the story would not reflect well on him."

Elizabeth lowered her head. "What does that signify? He can hardly consider me a lady now."

"Secondly," Charles said, stopping her with an upraised finger, "I am sure there are dozens of chaps who are dying to marry you."

"No, there are not," she said, impatiently shaking his hand away. "This is my fourth season and the only offers I have ever received have been from fortune seekers or doddering old cripples. It is quite apparent that I do not attract the right sort of man. Charlie, what is wrong with me?" She turned her tear-streaked face up to him again, and he made a great effort to answer her seriously and not give in to those same base instincts that Lord Westbridge had given in to earlier, although Charles knew very well *he* would not panic and run away afterwards.

"There is nothing wrong with you at all," he said in his most encouraging voice. "You are always one of the most popular girls at any affair. Why, I hardly ever have a chance to dance with you myself; your card is always filled up as soon as you enter the door."

"That is not quite true, Charlie," Elizabeth said in a

small voice, unfolding the handkerchief once more. "It is just that you always tread on my toes so dreadfully I sometimes tell you that my card is full when it is not. So you see, I am not nearly in as much demand as you think me."

"Nonsense—have you ever had to sit a dance out?"

"No," she admitted, "but what does that matter?"

"And are you not always the prettiest girl in the room?"

"How should I know? I do not spend all my time making comparisons," she replied airily.

"Then I will tell you so—you are always the prettiest girl in the room, in my opinion anyway."

"Thank you, Charlie," she said automatically. "You are so kind."

"I know plenty of fellows who would be honored to call you their wife."

"I don't believe you." She crinkled the handkerchief into a ball. "If that is so, why are they not perishing for love at my feet? I dare you to name me one."

Charles took a deep breath and looked her straight in the eyes. "Me, for example."

Elizabeth was so stunned it nearly took her breath away. "You, Charlie? *You?*" He nodded gravely, and she began to laugh.

He stood up abruptly and walked away from her. "If that is the way you greet a proposal of marriage, I do not wonder at your present difficulties."

Her laughter trailed off as she gazed at him in astonishment. "Do you mean you were actually proposing to me, Charlie? I can hardly believe it, it is too funny."

"That is quite evident without your telling me so," he said stiffly. "I withdraw the offer. I shouldn't want you to do yourself an injury by laughing too hard." He started for the door, but Elizabeth ran after him, placing a restraining hand upon his arm.

"I am sorry for laughing, Charlie. You took me by surprise, that is all. Please don't be cross," she pleaded

66

with him, and then seeing that he was softening, said, "Pax?"

He released his breath sharply. "Pax," he said.

"It is just that I never thought of you in that way," she explained, leading him back to the divan. "I mean, I have always thought of you as a friend, but never as a husband."

"That is not quite true," Charlie said, refusing to sit again. "We were engaged once, don't you remember?"

She creased her brow with the effort. "But we were only children then."

"You do remember." This was a statement, not a question.

"You were eight and I was six."

"That's right—it was the summer we spent at Thousand Acres."

"You were swinging on the gate and Emma pushed you off. You broke your ankle, and everyone thought I had done it, because Emma was always so little and mousy and never did anything like that," Elizabeth said quickly, as the memory of that day returned to her, sharp and clear. "I kept crying, 'I didn't do it! Emma did it!' but no one believed me and I was sent to my room, until you had recovered sufficiently to tell the truth."

"Which fortunately was that same afternoon."

"Yes, but it seemed like days to me." Elizabeth smiled. "I remember thinking how brave you were through the whole thing. There you were, lying on the ground, gone all white and pale—I thought for a moment you were dead—and you looked up at me and said, as calmly as though you were describing the weather, 'I think my ankle is broken—you'd better get someone to help.'"

Charlie leaned over and took her hand tenderly. "I don't remember that part very well, but I do remember how surprised and indignant I was when I learned Emma had told everyone it was *you* who had pushed me."

"I was always getting into trouble; of course they
67

thought I did it," Elizabeth said without bitterness. "And then I came and played with you every day while you recovered and we made all kinds of secret plans for when we would be married." She laughed a little. "But after that, you went away to school and I didn't see you again for three years. By then you had turned into a very nasty sort of person and I didn't want to marry you any more."

Charlie shuddered. "I wasn't really nasty—I was just going through my superior-to-thou stage in life. I didn't play with *girls*—that would have been beneath my dignity." He stroked her hand gently. "But deep down inside, that insufferable little prig I had turned into still wanted to marry you, Lizzie. And while I hope that I have improved with age, the offer still stands."

"It is very kind of you to say that, Charlie, but you needn't feel obliged to offer for me, just because you found me in a blue funk. I expect I shall recover one day." She sighed.

"I am offering for you only because I think it would be nice to be married to you." He deliberately made this an understatement, so she would not notice how anxious he really was. "I think we should suit."

"Perhaps we should," Elizabeth admitted; "but still— you go ahead and marry Emma if you want to."

It was Charlie's turn to laugh. "Whatever gave you the notion I wished to marry Emma?" he asked.

Elizabeth looked at him with surprise. "You were always supposed to marry Emma. Didn't your mother and Aunt Annabel make a pledge to that effect? We all knew about it. Even that summer, you and I had to keep our marriage plans secret because we knew you were promised to Emma."

Charlie shook his head, amused. "I had quite forgotten that ancient fancy of my mother's, but now that you have mentioned it, I do remember that I never considered it a good idea, even if it would put the estate back together."

"Well, Emma certainly has not forgotten," Elizabeth

told him. "She fully expects you to make good on that ancient fancy tonight."

Charlie's eyes narrowed. "Does she, by God?"

"She has talked of nothing else for the past week," Elizabeth said ruefully, thinking how often her own nose had been rubbed in Emma's expectations. "She is hoping to announce your engagement tonight, as the crowning moment of her ball."

"Is she, by God?" Charlie released her hand and began to pace restlessly. "Well, she certainly has given no hint of it to *me*. She has gone out of her way to be uncivil and contradict every statement I utter. Is that the behavior of a hopeful bride-to-be?"

"Perhaps she wishes to start as she means to go on," Elizabeth suggested. "Many wives treat their husbands just that way."

"And I don't intend to be one of them!" Charlie said with real anger. "Why, I don't even *like* the girl—I never have. In all the years I have known her I have never had a single intelligent conversation with her. And you are telling me that all this time she has believed that I would offer for her? Because of some silly promise made by our mothers when we were no more than babies?"

"Yes," Elizabeth said in a small voice, frightened by his anger.

"And has my aunt encouraged her in this notion?" he demanded.

"Oh, no," Elizabeth assured him. "She knows of it, but she is forever nagging Emma that she must treat you with more respect if she has any expectations of you."

"Her nagging has certainly had little effect."

"Charlie, please calm down. I have never seen you like this."

He managed to pause in his pacing and give her a grim smile. "No, you never have, for you have never seen me presented with an idea so abhorrent to me. I don't mean just the fact that Emma wishes to marry me—I suppose that is flattering in a way. But the very

69

idea that she knows me so little, knows practically nothing about me, and yet is so stolid and stupid that she is actually confident that I would wish to shackle myself to her—the very idea is infinitely repugnant to me." He noticed Elizabeth's bewildered expression and softened. "Forgive me, Lizzie; I suppose I have not completely outgrown an intolerance for stupidity. I still need to learn to make allowances for Emma's youth and faulty education."

There was a pause until Elizabeth said, "Don't you think we should be getting back to the ballroom? It must be nearly time for supper and we will be missed. Lord Westbridge was to take me in. . . ." She trailed off, thus reminded again of her own troubles.

"Look here, Lizzie," Charlie said brightly, taking her hands and standing her before him. "If you were to marry me it would be the solution to both our problems. Emma would be forced to look elsewhere and Westbridge would be thoroughly miffed that you took his rejection so lightly. I am not very good at fancy words—I should learn them out of books the way my friend Foxmoor does—but let me assure you that this is not the first time such a possibility has occurred to me. I simply never mentioned it before because I was sure you would react exactly as you did—by laughing in my face. But if once you recover from your laughter and can view my offer in a serious frame of mind, I would be most pleased if you would at least consider it. We may have had our differences, but at least we have always been friends, and that seems to me as good a basis for marriage as any."

They stood there for rather a long time, holding each other's hands and staring into each other's eyes, each of them thinking quite seriously indeed about what Charlie had proposed.

Charles himself was wondering if a dream he had had for years was about to come true. He knew very well the brotherly feelings Elizabeth entertained for him, but he flattered himself she was at least fond of him. That he loved her with more than a child's love was something he was not prepared to admit just yet; if he wooed her with flowery speeches and revealed to her the full depth of his regard, he feared he would scare her away. But there was a romantic streak in him that made him hope that given the opportunity, Elizabeth would learn to love him better.

Elizabeth's thoughts were of a much more practical nature. She had just suffered a thorough humiliation from Lord Westbridge, of that she was convinced. Despite Charlie's reassurances, she feared Westbridge would tell someone of her shame, and then the story would spread and she would be ruined forever. A respectable engagement for her would scotch all such rumors, and might even cause such intense feelings of regret in Westbridge's breast that he would come crawling back to her, begging her to break it off with Charlie and marry him.

And, of course, there was Emma to consider. Their betrothal would certainly take the wind out of *her* sails! Elizabeth smiled with satisfaction.

"Very well," she said at last. "I would be very pleased to become engaged to you, Charles."

He did not point out that he had asked her to marry him, not just become engaged. Most people considered an engagement nearly as binding as marriage. Even so, Charlie did not want an unwilling bride.

"If you should change your mind, Lizzie," he said softly, "if you should wake up tomorrow morning and realize that you acted too hastily, too rashly, then please tell me at once and I will release you from all obligation without rancor."

"Thank you, Charlie," she said. "That is very generous."

"In fact, I think it would be best if we waited until tomorrow to make any sort of announcement," he suggested.

"Are you afraid you, too, will be having second thoughts in the morning?" she asked whimsically.

"I? Never!" He embraced her briefly, not trusting

himself to do more than that. "I was merely giving one last thought to Emma's feelings in the matter."

"Yes, it would quite spoil her ball if we were to announce it now," Elizabeth said with a wicked smile.

"Yes, it would, and we are not going to do that, are we?" he said, a warning in his voice.

"Of course not!" Elizabeth avowed, as if the thought had never occurred to her.

"I will take you in to supper now," Charles said, offering her his arm.

"Thank you. I do not think Lord Westbridge would wish to claim me now," she said, as he led her out.

Emma Locke did not take the news of her cousins' betrothal graciously. She had gone to bed the night before with only a vague feeling of misgiving that Charles had not proposed to her as she had expected, comforting herself with the realization that she had been so much in demand that there had been no opportunity for him to take her aside and whisper the necessary words that would make her his. Secure with the knowledge that he would pay his respects on the morrow and ask for a conference with Mr. Locke during some point of his visit, she fell asleep happily, knowing that the evening had been a success.

Thus when Elizabeth did make her announcement at breakfast that morning, Emma was totally unprepared for it. For a few moments she stared blankly at Elizabeth, her jaw slack, wondering if this was just another of her cousin's cruel jests at her expense—and a pretty poor one at that. Then she heard the rest of her family greet the news quite seriously, with expressions of surprised congratulations, and she knew Elizabeth had spoken no more than the Dreadful Truth. All murmurs of congratulations were cut short when Emma gave a piercing wail, declared that she hated Elizabeth and everyone else in the world, and ran to her room in a stream of tears.

No one appeared unduly surprised by her outburst, for all had been privy to some degree to Emma's hopes regarding Charlie, but Mrs. Locke finally broke the uncomfortable silence that followed her daughter's exit by saying, quite matter-of-factly, "Emma has always been one to count her chickens before they are hatched. I have warned her against it time and again." She leaned across the table and patted Elizabeth's hand gently. "Never mind, my dear; be assured that we are all quite happy for you and dear Charles. I am sure Emma, too, will offer her congratulations when she returns to her senses." She folded her napkin and arose. "In the meantime, I must be a good mother and offer her some comfort and perhaps some I-told-you-so's as well. I can only hope that this will teach her a valuable lesson and show her how she may improve her behavior with young men she wishes to attract."

Mr. Locke did not wait long after his wife's departure to make his own. He was slightly confused by Emma's outburst, not being as fully acquainted with his daughter's hopes and desires as the others were, but he knew a good match when he saw one and said as much to Elizabeth.

"And," he added knowingly, "I know your father will be pleased, for he has always taken such an interest in the boy. You and Charlie will suit admirably. Good day, girls."

Francesca could barely contain herself until he had left the room, and as soon as the door was closed behind him she turned to Elizabeth with much distress.

"But what is this all about?" she asked. "What has happened to your plans regarding the oh-so-eligible marquess?"

Elizabeth sighed and gave her a rueful smile. "Francesca, it is all rather a great muddle and rather difficult to explain."

"I should think so! I thought your plan was to engage yourself to Lord Westbridge."

"And so it was," Elizabeth said with another sigh. "But that plan fell through." Briefly, she described the events of last night. "So when Charlie came in, and

73

asked me to marry *him* instead, it seemed like a good idea," she finished.

"I see," Francesca said thoughtfully. "But you are not in love with Charlie, are you?"

"I am very fond of him," Elizabeth said defensively.

"But you are still in love with Ivor," Francesca pursued.

Elizabeth nodded miserably, then looked down at her hands, ashamed.

"Never mind," Francesca said briskly. "I think I see how it will all come right in the end."

"How can it?" Elizabeth asked. "I am to marry Charlie."

"No, no, you are merely *engaged* to Charlie." Francesca had noticed this nice distinction immediately. "It could be considered an engagement of convenience—you know, like a marriage of convenience. You just told me yourself that it seemed the best solution to both your problems for the moment; perhaps a better solution will present itself in time." She folded her napkin and leaned in toward Elizabeth, as plans took shape in her mind. "Ivor will come to call—of this I have no doubt. And when he does, you let me talk to him. He will become so mad with desire for you that he will stop at nothing to marry you."

"How can you be so sure?" Elizabeth asked her suspiciously.

"I just am," Francesca assured her. "Leave everything to me."

Her excitement was contagious, and Elizabeth felt a happy bubble of anticipation rise within her. Yes, she thought decidedly, with Francesca's help she could take control of her own life again and everything would turn out right.

# SIX

Lord Westbridge certainly did not enjoy the rest of the ball, nor did he sleep well that night. Too late had he realized why Miss Durant had wished to be alone with him, too late had he discovered that the speck of dust in her eye was no more than a fiction to make him do exactly as he had done—to become carried away and kiss her. He knew, too, what should have come after that kiss as well as Miss Durant herself knew, but she had taken him by surprise; he was not yet prepared to take that step from which there is no retreat. His combat-ready alertness had left him in these years of peace; left him when he was most in need of it.

At first he was angry—with himself for falling into the trap and with Miss Durant for setting it. This anger carried over to his behavior with the other young ladies with whom he was engaged to dance that night, and after snubbing two such unsuspecting maidens most vilely, he thought it best to remove himself from the premises completely. Fortunately, he did not run into Miss Durant again, for if he had he would not have known what to say to her.

In the comfort of his sitting room at home, with a glass of port by his side and a small but cheerful fire crackling in the hearth, his anger subsided and he actually began to wonder why he had not indeed taken his cue when it was offered him. Miss Durant was certainly not unattractive to him; he had been very seriously considering making her his bride—she was high on his list of candidates for the position and had been from the very start. She was undoubtedly beautiful, had a small fortune and great presence; a coronet would not look awry on those golden curls. He had already passed several very pleasant evenings in her company, and knew quite well that she returned his regard. Most important, if he had asked Miss Durant to be his wife, which was obviously her desire, he would have been released from the necessity of pursuing anyone else and would have been free to spend evenings at his club once more or make a long-overdue visit to Soho. His duty would have been discharged, and promptly, too, and he was quite certain his father would have been pleased by his choice.

The more he thought about it, the more the idea of marriage to Miss Durant appealed to him. A dozen more points in her favor occurred to him as he sat there, sipping his wine, and not a point against; and as her score mounted to impressive heights, his anger was gradually replaced by an uncomfortable prickling of his conscience. He had behaved badly. He had kissed Miss Durant with no thought beyond the momentary pleasure it would afford him, and when the opportunity was given him to make good on the promise of that kiss, he had beaten a hasty and ignoble retreat. That was behavior unbecoming an officer. If he had acted so crassly on the field of battle, Napoleon would never have been defeated and might even now be emperor over England herself.

This thought was not to be borne. Ivor arose, refilled his glass, and began pacing restlessly. In his mind, a stolen kiss had now taken on the proportions of treason to his country and a denial of all the values he had ever held dear, the dearest of which was Honor itself. Was that not the motto on the Westham coat of arms? *Honos Est Omnis*—Honor Is All. Why, he had behaved

76

no better than his brother Ingram, disgracing his name and his nation, plunging his family into yet another scandal of hideous proportions. He had known very well what his duty was and had thought he was pursuing it diligently; but when the opportunity to execute that duty had been presented to him, he had shirked it. He was not fit to be called a Westham, not fit for the honorary title of Marquess of Westbridge, and certainly not fit to inherit the honorable and revered title of Duke of Duxton.

He refilled his glass and came to a decision. He would call upon Miss Durant in the morning and discover how agreeable she would be to a proposal of marriage. If she was agreeable, he would speak to her uncle and write to her father and, of course, consult his own father, too. He would do the Honorable thing, he would cause the family name to be used as a pattern of all that was right and just within England's shores. *Honos Est Omnis!*

It was nearly light and the decanter was nearly empty by the time Ivor finally went to bed, and when he was awakened by his man only a few hours later, he was in a befuddled state of mind. It took him a few minutes to remember his resolution of the night before, but once reminded he was full of action. The first thing he did was write a letter to Gerald Durant, Elizabeth's father, stating his intentions and requesting the traditional parental blessings. He was nothing if not thorough, and listed his titles, awards, and achievements as well as his current and future income. No father could refuse such a noble suitor, and Ivor felt very much better after he had seen this missive posted. Let it not be said that he was one who refused to right a wrong.

He then presented himself at the Lockes' residence, feeling almost as he had when victory over the French was assured. In his confidence, he forgot about the Hundred Days that had soon followed the first peace, and did not realize that he was in for a similar setback in his own fortunes.

He was ushered into the sitting room, where Miss Durant and Miss DelSorro were pursuing their needlework. He was not of an artistic nature or he might have paused a moment to admire the picture they made, the one so dark, the other so fair, the morning light haloing the two heads poised delicately on two very elegant necks. But this picture lasted only a second, else he might have admired it eventually, for as soon as he entered Miss Durant put aside her work and rose to greet him.

"What a very unexpected pleasure to see you this morning, my lord," she said, a faint pinkness creeping into her cheeks. "I hope you enjoyed the ball last night."

"A very pleasant evening," he replied automatically, taking her hand and bowing over it. He then nodded to Francesca. "Miss DelSorro, always a pleasure."

"Indeed," Francesca murmured, a slight smile twitching at the corners of her mouth.

"Won't you sit down," Elizabeth invited, indicating with a graceful wave of her hand which seat he should occupy.

"Thank you," he replied, taking his place and wiping his palms surreptitiously on the arms of the chair so that the ladies would not be aware of his nervousness. "Miss Locke does not sit with you?" he asked after a moment.

"She has been taken ill," Miss DelSorro explained. "The exertions of last night . . . you understand. . . ." She trailed off.

"Yes, of course." Lord Westbridge wondered frantically how it might be possible to speak to Elizabeth alone without being unduly rude to Miss DelSorro, but before he could think of how this might be managed, Miss Durant spoke again.

"My lord, you may be one of the first to congratulate me," she said, her voice unnaturally high. "I have become engaged to Mr. Buckley."

Ivor stared at her blankly, unable to absorb the

significance of her remark. Elizabeth stared back for a few moments, bravely meeting his eyes until suddenly her courage failed her.

"I am so sorry," she said at last, arising again. "I fear the exertions of last evening were a little too much for me as well. Francesca, you would not think it terribly rude of me if I left you alone to entertain Lord Westbridge, would you?"

"Of course not," Francesca said with an approving nod to her cousin, and Elizabeth murmured a farewell to Lord Westbridge and left them alone.

Ivor stared at the door for some moments after Elizabeth closed it behind her, hardly able to believe what he had just heard. Finally he broke away to look at Miss DelSorro with a helpless glance.

"I don't understand," he said.

"No, indeed, but you should," Francesca said matter-of-factly. "You have made a great cake of yourself." When he gave her a look of surprise she added seriously, "Is that not the correct expression?"

"I—I am not certain. It depends upon what you mean by it." He was clearly uncomfortable, for despite his stated preference for plainspoken ladies, he had not really had all that much experience with them.

Francesca smoothed her skirt carefully. "Let me tell you then that my cousin has confided in me the events of last night— Wait! Before you leave in a puff, let me assure you that I am her only confidante and that you may rely utterly on my discretion."

Lord Westbridge resumed his seat, which he had recently vacated upon Miss DelSorro's first words.

"Might it be amiss of me," Francesca inquired, "to ask you exactly why you chose to call upon my cousin this morning?"

"I don't see that—it really makes no difference—it was just—a matter of honor is always—well, she has become engaged now anyway, so it doesn't matter one way or the other," he finished lamely.

Francesca nodded wisely. "Just as I thought! You

came here to propose to her. Quite right, I admire your courage. You had time to reflect upon your dastardly behavior of last night and decided to do the proper thing. It was very well thought of you, but as you see you are too late." She raised her hand as Ivor showed signs of leaving again. "My lord—El Colonel." He looked at her curiously, and she smiled. "Yes, I would prefer to address you as my old friend, El Colonel. Do you not recall how I used to admire all your shiny buttons and how I sneaked away from my lessons to come and watch you march in the square? And I tried always to sit next to you at dinner, that is, when I was allowed to join you. You always looked so smart in your red coat."

"Miss DelSorro—"

"Doña Francesca, please, as you used to."

"Doña Francesca, it would be very pleasant to sit and reminisce with you over old times, but I am afraid my state of mind at the moment would not permit it." He bowed his head briefly, as if summoning up the strength to decide what to do next.

"It is not my intention to sit and chat idly with you," Francesca said. "I merely brought that up so you will not be offended when I speak to you quite frankly."

Ivor was decidedly uncomfortable and not at all certain he wished to be spoken to quite frankly. What he chiefly needed was some time alone to think, for a most perplexing question had occurred to him: How was Honor to be satisfied when the lady was already betrothed to another?

"El Colonel, a dreadful wrong has been done," Francesca said, the apparent prelude to her frank talk. "My cousin—"

Ivor came to a decision. The Marquess of Westbridge was not one to sit quietly and take an upbraiding from a woman! "Miss DelSorro," he interrupted haughtily, "I appreciate your interest, but must point out that my responsibility in the matter has ended now that Miss Durant is betrothed to another." He arose and drew himself to his full height, looking down his nose at her. "I came here to do the honorable thing, but now that I have discovered it is unnecessary, I will take my leave of you."

"You are quite right, my lord; it was wrong of me to presume so," Francesca said, her tone contrite. "Let me ring for the servant to see you out." But she stopped before she had reached her goal and turned to him. "El Colonel, máy I ask you a question—about a point of honor?"

"Certainly," he said graciously.

"You must understand that these things are exceedingly difficult for me—a mere woman—to comprehend." She gave him an apologetic smile.

Lord Westbridge returned the smile indulgently.

"Now let me see if I have this right," she continued. "You came here today to propose to my cousin because you took advantage of her last night, is that correct?"

He reluctantly acknowledged that this was so.

"Such behavior was dishonorable on your part, and you wished to do the honorable thing to rectify the situation." She spoke slowly, to be quite certain she got it right. "Then tell me, El Colonel, why is it *not* dishonorable to force a lady into an unhappy marriage because of that same dishonorable act?"

"I beg your pardon?" He had lost the thread of the argument.

"My cousin will not be happy with Mr. Buckley, for she is still in love with you," Francesca said simply. "In effect, you are the cause of all the unhappiness she will suffer in her future life, and yet you consider that your responsibility has ended. That does not quite make sense to me. Please explain." She inclined her head to him, awaiting his reply. "Understand," she added, "that I ask merely for the information, not to imply that you are in any way answerable for Elizabeth's happiness or lack of it."

Lord Westbridge tried to comply with her request. Several times he opened his mouth, only to shut it

81

again before anything but air could pass through his lips. Finally he sat down again, his shoulders bowed in defeat.

"But what is to be done? I have already acted dishonorably, I cannot add to that dishonor by stealing her away from her betrothed."

"Is it dishonorable if she wishes to be stolen?" Francesca asked. "I do not understand these things myself, so I do wish you would tell me if I am entirely wrong in my suppositions."

"You are quite certain she will be unhappy with Mr. Buckley?" he asked, after pondering the problem at great length.

Francesca shrugged. "How does one know anything for sure in this life? What I do know is that she accepted him only because she had been humiliated by you. I am sorry, El Colonel, but I told you I would speak frankly." She sighed. "But, as you say, you cannot make things better by acting dishonorably again. Is not the English expression 'Two wrongs do not make a right'?"

"But something must be done!" he exclaimed, pounding his fists on the arms of the chair for emphasis. "I cannot let her marry Buckley; I would not be able to live with myself. He is a short, nearsighted dullard, with conversation as interesting as an encyclopedia."

"Ah, you know Charlie," Francesca said.

"Doña Francesca," he said, rising again and moving toward her, "can you advise me what to do? You know your cousin well, I suppose?"

"I have known her but a week, but we have become friends," she told him.

"Then tell me what to do. What are her feelings in the matter? How can I win her back and give her the happiness she deserves?"

"What I say to you you will hold in the strictest confidence, of course?"

"That is understood," Ivor said, mildly offended.

"Very well then, Elizabeth is one who likes the romance and excitement," she said carefully. "Last

82

night perhaps she found it romantic and exciting to engage herself to Charles, but it will not take her long to realize her mistake, if indeed she has not done so already. It will take her even less time if you are nearby for her to make the comparison. My advice to you is not to give up hope. Try to meet her as often as possible, take her driving, send her nosegays and buy her small presents of books. In this way she will learn that you care for her, and will break off her engagement of her own accord, with no dishonor on your part."

Ivor regarded her gratefully, impressed by the beautiful simplicity of her solution. "You have been most kind, Francesca, in telling me all this."

"Not at all, El Colonel." She smiled. "When the fates of two people I hold dear are at stake, there is nothing I would not do to ensure their happiness." At last she pulled the bell cord to summon Jenkins to see Lord Westbridge out.

He held out his hands to her, and she clasped them warmly.

"I hope you will always feel free to turn to me for advice in the future," she said. "That is, should things not seem to progress to your liking."

"I certainly will," he said with feeling. "I am ready to do anything to have Miss Durant look upon me with favor once more."

"Keep that in mind, El Colonel, for it may come to that," Francesca said with a warning note in her voice, "if the first part of our plan does not proceed as expected."

A few minutes after he had left, Elizabeth returned to the sitting room, eager to discover what Lord Westbridge and Francesca had been talking of for so long, but the news was disappointing.

"We spoke mostly of the time we knew each other in Madrid," Francesca told her placidly, picking up her needlework and taking a few stitches. "And then we had quite a philosophical discussion about honor."

"Then you do not think he came to propose to me?" Elizabeth asked her.

"Oh, he undoubtedly did, although he did not say as much to me. But I believe his interest in you is stronger than ever—he was most distressed by the news of your betrothal."

"Then what am I to do?" Elizabeth asked, throwing herself disconsolately into a chair.

"My advice to you is wait and see," Francesca said without hesitation. "It does not hurt to have more than one man dangling after you." She folded her embroidery neatly and put it into her workbox. "But now I must go and change. Mr. Davis is taking me for a drive this afternoon, and he is always most punctual."

In the week that followed, Elizabeth discovered that it *was* quite pleasant to have more than one gentleman dangling after her. In fact, it was quite amazing to her how Lord Westbridge's attentions had increased with the knowledge that she was engaged to another, but outside of wondering whether he had at last fallen in love with her, she did not ponder long the whys and wherefores of his behavior, for she was too busy enjoying it. He always approached her moments after entering a room, always with some compliment upon his lips and requests for a dance or two. When she visited the theater, he came to her box during the interval, and he finally invited her out for a drive one afternoon. This episode was one of the most pleasant hours they passed together, and Elizabeth felt proud to be in his company. He was so worldly and self-assured, and attracted admiring glances wherever he went.

Charles Buckley was not blind to Westbridge's increased interest in Elizabeth, but thought it best to keep his mouth shut for the time being. He was well aware that their engagement was a tentative thing, and would not have come about at all if this Westbridge fellow had offered first. That he did not like the man was an opinion he kept to himself; that he did not like the way the man was treating Elizabeth was an opinion more difficult to hide. On more than one occasion he had to struggle to keep a civil tongue in his head when Westbridge as good as whisked Elizabeth out from under his very nose. His consolation was in the belief that the more time Elizabeth spent with the man, the sooner she would learn that Westbridge was a puffed-up popinjay, full of conceit and completely lacking a sense of humor. Charlie knew it was dangerous to rely on Elizabeth's own sense of humor to help her see through the man, but it was all he could do for now.

Elizabeth herself was confused by her feelings. She had believed at first that a single word from Westbridge would send her flying to Charlie to break it off, but gradually, despite her undying love for Westbridge, she began to realize it would take more than a mere word. To her surprise, she soon discovered that she liked spending time with Charlie, too, and they seemed to be spending a great deal of time together now, for he always came to call in the morning and frequently came to dinner or tea. Elizabeth felt comfortable with him; he had known her all her life and had seen her at her worst, so she was not always compelled to be on her best behavior, but could say whatever she liked without fear of offending. She could argue with him or contradict him, and he wouldn't mind a bit; he would merely point out with infinite patience where she was mistaken, or cheerfully admit himself wrong. And Charlie always made her laugh. Elizabeth acknowledged with some regret that Lord Westbridge rarely laughed, and while she admired his serious attitude toward life, she could not help but view his lack of humor as a failing.

But even Charles Buckley's patience was not infinite, and after several more weeks of Elizabeth's blowing hot and cold, it was finally stretched to the limits.

He came one afternoon to collect her for a drive. She did not often go driving with him, for she doubted his skill and did not think too much of his horses, either, but she had had no other engagements for that afternoon and did have some errands in the shops, so she had suggested to Charlie the night before that she wouldn't mind driving out with him just this once.

He presented himself promptly as usual, and Elizabeth greeted him alone in the sitting room.

"Oh, Charlie, I shan't be needing you after all, for Ivor said he might call and take me through the park."

"What?" Charlie said shortly, hardly able to believe his ears.

"But there are some books waiting for me at the circulating library. If you are going that way you might pick them up for me, there's a dear."

"I thought we were to go out together," Charles said, and his tightened jaw should have been a warning to her.

"I just told you—Lord Westbridge said he might call," Elizabeth said with a flash of impatience.

"Yes, that is what I thought you said. Fetch your hat and let us go."

"Is there something wrong with your hearing, Charlie? I have told you I cannot go with you."

"There is obviously something wrong with your memory. We had an engagement. Are you trying to tell me you are going to break it because some self-important jackanapes *might* call? Fetch your hat now!"

"Just because you don't like him—"

"Do you want me to fetch your hat for you? I don't think it will take me too long to discover your bedroom. It will be the one with all the clothes lying about in heaps because you couldn't make up your mind what to wear!" He started for the door.

"No, no, I will get it," she cried out hastily.

She returned shortly, her hat upon her head and a shawl about her shoulders.

"I left a message for Ivor," she said glumly. "This is really too bad of you, Charlie."

He did not reply, but led her out to his awaiting phaeton, dismissed his groom, and handed Elizabeth into the carriage. Then he took his place beside her and took up the reins, and they were off for their pleasant

86

afternoon drive with all the joy and happiness of two members of a cortège.

"You are going the wrong way," Elizabeth remarked presently.

"No, I am not. I wish to talk to you. I am going where we can talk."

"We could have talked at home," she said petulantly, "and then I would have been there when Ivor called."

"If you mention that name once more I will turn you out of the carriage and you can walk home," Charlie told her severely.

"Ivor, Ivor, Ivor," Elizabeth chanted childishly, but Charles did not make good on his threat.

In another quarter hour they were out in the countryside, and Charles pulled the horses over to the side. Elizabeth stared resolutely away from him, determined that she would not utter a word until she was home once more.

"Look here, Lizzie, are we engaged to be married or not?"

Silence.

"Why have you not yet sent the announcement to the paper? You keep promising you will do so."

Silence.

"If you want to break it off, just tell me so. I am sure I do not want to lead you kicking and screaming to the altar."

Silence.

He sighed. "I haven't heard from your father yet, Lizzie, and I wrote him nearly a month ago."

"Do not call me Lizzie."

"For God's sake, Lizzie, what is wrong with you? We are not little children playing a game any more, we are discussing the rest of our lives. That means forever, as we know it in this world. Now, if you want to marry me, that is fine, but if you have changed your mind I would appreciate it if you would let me know."

He sounded exasperated, and Elizabeth was suddenly ashamed.

"I'm sorry, Charlie," she said in a small voice. "I acted like a pig, you have every right to be angry with me."

Charles put his hand under her chin and lifted her face. "But you still have not answered my question—do you want to marry me or not?"

"I said I would," she replied, unable to meet his eyes.

"Then you have not changed your mind?"

"I don't think so."

He pulled away from her. "And what *do* you think? That you can keep me hanging on a string until you are sure of your precious Ivor? *You* don't have a thing to worry about; if Ivor doesn't come to the point there is always good old Charlie."

"No—I—it is not like that at all," Elizabeth protested, the aptness of his comments causing her to object more strongly than if there had been no truth in them at all. "A week," she said at last. "Give me a week, Charlie. I promise you I will come to a definite decision by then."

He sighed. "Very well, a week then." He took up the reins and started the horses back to town. "I think we still have time to do those errands of yours, if you like."

But the weather did not agree with them, for there was a rumble of thunder in the distance and in a very few minutes the rain was pouring down upon them.

Charlie tried to hurry the horses, but the road quickly turned to slippery mud, so their progress was necessarily slow.

"Thank goodness I am wearing this old hat," Elizabeth shouted, the noise of the rain and thunder nearly drowning out her voice. "It will be quite ruined."

"You mean you didn't put on your best hat for me?" Charlie shouted back.

"Of course not. I was angry with you," she laughed.

If only the conditions of the road had not required all of his attention, he might have dropped the reins then and there and kissed her beautiful laughing face. If he had known how much trouble would have been avoided

88

by such an action on his part, he would have kissed her in any case, even if it landed them in a ditch. But he was blithely unaware of what was to befall them all in the near future, and so once again he resisted the impulse, guiding the horses carefully until they were safely back on Upper Grosvenor Street.

# SEVEN

*Elizabeth, my dear,*

*I hope this letter finds you well, but considering the reason I write I expect you are more than well. In fact, it seems to me that you must be blooming, and perhaps that is why you are so behindhand in your correspondence.*

*However, I am not writing to inquire after your health. Several weeks ago I received two very interesting letters, both by the same post, and both containing the same request—your hand in marriage. I opened the letter from Charles Buckley first, not realizing its significance right away, for he started out in his usual style. I was most delighted to learn of your engagement to him, but I confess this delight turned to confusion when I opened the second letter, which was from Lord Westbridge, asking for my blessings upon his engagement to you.*

*Elizabeth, I realize that I have never dictated to you, even though as your father it is my right to do so. I have always allowed you to make your own decisions, trusting to your good sense that they will be the right ones. That is why it distresses me mightily to learn that you seem to have engaged yourself to two gentlemen at once. Surely, even in the freedom of today's world, that is not the thing to do.*

*Both gentlemen requested my reply by return post, but as I could not think of what to say to either of them,*

*I put the task off as long as possible, until I realized it would be most expedient to write directly to you. Even if you are engaged to two men at once, you cannot marry them both; therefore you must make a choice (unless you have converted to a new religion that allows polygamy and have neglected to communicate that information to me as well). It is not my intention to direct that choice, for I know you will do as you please despite what I say, but while I have little hope that my preference will influence you one way or the other, it is at least my duty as a parent to indicate that preference to you.*

*Lord Westbridge writes most eloquently, describing in detail what he can offer you through marriage, which is much. It would doubtless be a very fine thing for you to be a duchess one day, and I would be proud to see you in that station. If you choose Westbridge, rest assured that your marriage will have my blessing.*

*However, I cannot help but admit that I would prefer to see you marry Charles. He had no reason to list his prospects, since as his former guardian I am already well acquainted with them. Except for the title, they are in every way comparable to those of Lord Westbridge. Nonetheless, I am prejudiced in Charlie's favor. He is a fine young man for whom I have always had a great fondness; his academic accomplishments are impressive, as is his athletic skill. He has a generous nature, a sharp wit, and a sense of justice I think would be indispensable in a husband. Also, I believe he would suit you better than Lord Westbridge, being much closer in age to you and sharing a similar background. Perhaps you think it odd of me to mention such a thing as age, as Anna is so much younger than I, but it is, at least, one of the points you should take into consideration in making your choice.*

*I do hope you will make your decision quickly, for I cannot think it can be comfortable to be engaged to two people at once, from a strictly social point of view. It must be awkward to seat the three of you at dinner*

*parties. I hope you will plan an autumn wedding, for
that would be most convenient for us. Anna increases
in size daily and has about a month of her time to go.
By the autumn both she and the baby should be well
enough to travel with me to London to see you wed.*

*My regards to all the Lockes.*

Your loving father,
Gerald Durant

Francesca handed the letter back to Elizabeth, saying,
"Your father is a very generous man."

"But don't you see the point, Francesca?" Elizabeth
said excitedly. "I had no idea Ivor had already written
to Father."

"A most encouraging sign," Francesca said. "What
will you do?"

"I don't know," Elizabeth admitted. "Every day it
becomes more difficult for me to make up my mind, for
every day I see a new fault in Ivor and a new virtue in
Charles." She gave an exasperated sigh. "I used to
think that Ivor was such a dashing figure—just like a
handsome prince out of a storybook—but some of his
notions are so antiquated it makes me despair of him.
He never seeks my opinion on any subject, and when I
offer one he smiles indulgently and pats my hand, as
though I had just said something quite adorable but
with no meaning, like a performing parrot."

"That is a fault that can be corrected in time,"
Francesca pointed out. "You can soon demonstrate to him
that your opinions carry weight—after you are married."

"I suppose so." Elizabeth sighed. "But worse than
that, I am afraid he has no notion of having *fun*. When
we were driving through the park the other day, I
mentioned how much I enjoyed skating in the winter in
the counryside when the streams are frozen over, and
he said skating was a most unhealthful activity and
that he ventured out as little as possible in the cold
weather! Imagine! That from a man who spent entire
winters out of doors when he was in the army!"

"There is no snow in Spain," Francesca pointed out. "But Lord Westbridge is a fine sportsman, nonetheless. Is he not a member of the Four Hands Club?"

"The Four-in-Hand Club," Elizabeth corrected. "Yes, that is true. Just as it is true that my heart beats faster whenever I see him and that I count every minute I am parted from him. I love him to despair, Francesca, but I think I would love him even more if once, just once, he did something rash. I would like to know he was the kind of man who would sweep me off my feet and carry me away because he was dying of love for me. The kind of man who would fight a duel for me. He needn't make a habit of it, of course," she added generously. "Just once is all I ask."

"I am certain he would be the kind of man to fight a duel, if his honor was at stake," Francesca said decidedly.

"But what about *my* honor?" Elizabeth wailed. "Oh, Francesca, what is wrong with me? I always thought that when I fell in love I would have no doubts at all about it, and that the man I loved would be ever so passionately in love with me. Ivor is so much a stickler for propriety that I can hardly picture him ever doing anything without thinking long and hard about the consequences beforehand."

"That is what made him a good soldier," Francesca told her.

Elizabeth looked at the letter from her father and sighed yet again. "Perhaps I should just please Father and marry Charlie after all. We would have a comfortable life together, I suppose, and I *am* fond of him, and he of me. I wonder what Father means about his impressive athletic skill," she murmured, rereading the letter. "Charlie has never impressed me as being particularly athletic."

Francesca was quietly self-absorbed at the moment and did not hear Elizabeth's last remark. Finally, with a quick, sharp nod of her head she looked up at Elizabeth with a calculating gleam in her eye.

"I must go out and do some errands, Elizabeth," she said. "Is there anything you need in the shops?"

"No," Elizabeth replied. "Would you like me to come with you? I have nothing planned for this afternoon."

"That will not be necessary," Francesca said quickly. "Conchita will accompany me. I think you should go upstairs and rest, Elizabeth. It seems to me you have been thinking too hard, and that is bad for the brain, to say nothing of your looks. Do we not attend the theater this evening?"

"I believe it is *Twelfth Night*," Elizabeth said without enthusiasm. "I have seen it before."

"But both your young men will be there," Francesca said, "so you must rest and remove that worried expression from your face."

Elizabeth agreed to the wisdom of this advice, and as she was leaving the room, Emma came in. It had taken the girl only a day or two to recover from Elizabeth's engagement to Charlie. A heart-to-heart talk with her mother, who had pointed out that it was silly of Emma to give up all hope the very day after her debut in society, did much to restore her self-confidence, and it was not long before she discovered, to her delight, that Charles Buckley was not the only eligible bachelor in London—indeed, far from it. There were many young men who appeared quite eager for an introduction to her, and it was a rare evening indeed that she sat out more than two dances with the dowagers and matrons on the side. Of course, her first evening at Almack's was something of a disappointment, for the refreshments were not at all what she was used to, but this momentary discomfort was allayed by the fact that here she met absolutely dozens of men, all of them seeking wives. She felt confident that she would not end her first season without having received at least one proposal of marriage and very likely accepting it.

However, she had still not forgiven Elizabeth for her setback in this regard, and was not really on speaking terms with her cousin. Thus Emma gave her barely a nod when Elizabeth passed through the door on her way upstairs.

"Emma, I *am* glad to see you," Francesca said. This cheered Emma up considerably, for she was somewhat jealous of her cousins' friendship, which usually excluded her.

"I find I must go on an urgent errand," Francesca continued. "I was engaged to drive out with Mr. Foxmoor this afternoon. Do you think you might convey my apologies to him and perhaps entertain him in my stead?"

"I would be happy to," Emma said truthfully. She liked Mr. Foxmoor and liked even better this opportunity to steal one of Francesca's suitors for herself, and quite a handsome one at that.

Francesca left shortly afterwards with her maid, and Emma watched them go without curiosity, for she was eager for the arrival of Mr. Foxmoor. She primped in the looking glass, making sure that her hair was in place and pinching her cheeks to make them glow a rosy red. This was hardly necessary, for Emma had naturally a most healthy complexion with nary a freckle or blemish, she noted to her satisfaction.

By the time Nigel Foxmoor arrived and was shown into the sitting room, Emma had become quite bright-eyed and pink with anticipation.

"Mr. Foxmoor, this is indeed a pleasure," she said, extending her hand graciously. "I am afraid Miss DelSorro is unable to keep your engagement this afternoon. She sends her apologies and hopes that you will be content with my company for the moment."

"My pleasure, Miss Locke," he said, taking the seat she indicated for him. He was slightly disappointed and decided that he would stay only for the regulation quarter hour, long enough to exchange a few words with Miss Locke and think of a suitable message to leave for Miss DelSorro.

Emma offered him refreshment, which he refused, and they began chatting, Emma commenting once again on the beauty of his carriage and pair. He went into the now familiar description of how he had obtained such a fine turnout, explaining once more in detail why he felt it was always necessary to match the color of the carriage to the color of the horses. Emma listened raptly, giving no indication that she had heard the tale before, and indeed she delighted in the retelling, for Mr. Foxmoor did speak so beautifully and with such resonance and she was completely in sympathy with his notions of fashion.

"Yes, color is very important," she agreed with him gravely, when the opportunity presented itself, "especially in matters of style. For example, I have always felt that I would appear to greater advantage in deeper, brighter hues, but society dictates that I should wear only the palest pastels and white. It is very boring."

"I can picture you in shades of green, Miss Locke," Nigel said, warming to the subject. "Your eyes have a greenish cast to them, and if you wore a green dress, it might bring that feature out."

"Do you think my eyes are green? I always considered them pale blue."

"And so they are—in this light, and against that white frock you are wearing. But they are pale enough that they catch the reflections of other colors around them. Yes, I believe I am right—green is the color for you, and I will tell you the truth, it is not very many women who can wear green. It makes their skin appear sallow, you see. But you haven't a hint of sallowness, I am glad to say."

"You are most kind, Mr. Foxmoor, and I will certainly heed your advice, if Mama will allow me to." She smiled, showing off her dimples. "I know exactly what you mean about turning the skin yellow, too. Did you happen to notice Lady Blaine the other evening? She had on a gown of jade silk and I swear when I first saw her I thought she was sickening for something!"

"Quite so! I thought exactly the same!" Nigel exclaimed happily. They went on in this way for some time, each with an amazingly accurate memory of what was worn by every lady or gentleman at every function they had attended. When Nigel glanced at the clock he was surprised to note that quite half an hour had passed already.

"Look here," he said suddenly, as a happy thought occurred to him. "I was supposed to take Miss DelSorro for a drive with me, but as she is not here I do wonder if you might honor me with your presence instead—since you have expressed such admiration for my carriage."

"I would love to." Emma laughed, a delicate, tinkling laugh like little silver bells chiming. Her mother would have been much pleased by that sound and taken note of its significance. She had spent years to no effect trying to cure Emma's horsy bray; Nigel Foxmoor had accomplished the task in a single afternoon.

In a very few minutes Miss Locke had the extreme pleasure of traveling through the park in just about the finest carriage on display there, seated next to a man who was certainly the most handsome in London. If Elizabeth and Francesca could only see her now they would both turn quite as green as Lady Blaine.

That evening the Lockes attended the theater, accompanied by Mr. Buckley and Mr. Foxmoor, who was now torn in his loyalties. He had learned by heart another passage from one of his Gothic romances that described Miss DelSorro most aptly, but he could never seem to find the opportunity to use it. Every time he opened his mouth to speak, something happened to interrupt him; Miss DelSorro saw another gentleman whom she couldn't possibly snub, or the curtain rose on the performance and he was perfunctorily hushed. During the interval, their box was so jammed with other young men seeking her attentions that he saw no hope of reciting his piece that evening. Then a voice piped up behind him.

"Mr. Foxmoor, I rely on your taste exceedingly. Do tell me what you thought of Viola's costume—did you not find it rather vulgar, as I did? Trousers are simply not becoming to a woman's figure."

He turned to Miss Locke eagerly, and after they had discussed all of the costumes, bethought himself of a passage he had particularly liked about an English milkmaid, toothsome and rosy, which he believed was Miss Locke to the letter.

Elizabeth Durant, too, had a piece she longed to speak to a certain party, but the opportunity never presented itself. Lord Westbridge did come to their box during the second interval, but Elizabeth had no chance to ask him why he had not told her he had written to her father. She was afforded a different opportunity, though, and that was to observe Charles and Ivor side by side. Charles suffered much by the comparison. Ivor was a good six inches taller and had an impressive breadth of shoulder to go with his height. Where Charlie was fair and pleasant-looking, Ivor was swarthy and rugged, and it could not be denied that Charlie's spectacles gave him a decidedly owlish look.

Elizabeth thought about this comparison again that night as she lay in her bed, waiting for sleep to come. Also, she thought of the great number of significant glances Ivor had directed to her and his whispered "I must speak with you, Miss Durant" just before they had parted. If the subject he wished to discuss was the same one that had consumed Elizabeth's thoughts for the last month, her decision was made. She would marry Ivor.

Their opportunity to speak did not come until the next night, at the Worthings' ball. Ivor had led Elizabeth out for the first dance but did not then draw her aside, as it would have been too much noticed by the rest of the company. Instead he waited until he saw Elizabeth step out into the garden for a breath of air and chose that moment to follow her there.

"Miss Durant?" he said softly, coming up behind her where she leaned against a railing, gazing at the moon.

"My lord," she said with a start. "Forgive me, I did not hear you approach."

"I did not mean to alarm you, Elizabeth."

"Of course not, you could never do that—Ivor." It was the first time she had spoken his Christian name to him, although she used it always in her thoughts, and she spoke it tentatively.

"My dear Elizabeth, it has occurred to me that while I have seen you any number of times since, I have never properly apologized to you for my callous behavior at your cousin's ball."

"There is no need, Ivor. It is I who should apologize to you. I was most forward." She bowed her head.

"No, no, I insist that I was the one to blame, for I did not know then what I know now."

"And what is that, my lord?" she whispered, looking up at him expectantly.

"That I wish to marry you—if you will have me."

Elizabeth felt her heart in her throat and had to swallow deeply before she could reply, "Oh yes, please."

He placed his hands in the railing and looked out on the garden. "I have written to your father for his permission, but have heard no reply."

"I know," she said.

"You knew that?" He looked at her, surprised. "How did you discover it? I told no one."

"I heard from my father yesterday. He apologized for not writing to you directly, but Mr. Buckley had written to him with the same request, so he wished to leave the decision to me. He looks with favor upon your suit," she told him happily. "So you need have no reservations on that score."

"That is good," Lord Westbridge said. "But what of Buckley? Are you engaged to him or not?"

"Oh, Charlie will not mind," Elizabeth assured him blithely. "We only decided to become engaged because it seemed a good idea at the time, but now circumstances have changed."

"Then there is nothing to stop you marrying me?" he asked, taking her hand.

99

"Nothing at all," she told him happily.

"Then come away with me now."

"What?" Elizabeth was taken aback by his impetuosity.

"Come away with me now, this minute, Elizabeth, for I cannot wait another day for you. I have a coach ready and a special license in my pocket. We can be at Westham Park by tomorrow afternoon if we start tonight, and wed the next day with the license."

Elizabeth could hardly believe her ears. This was actually the proper and thoughtful Lord Westbridge who was telling her that he wished to sweep her off her feet and carry her away, just as she had longed for him to do!

Yet she hesitated. "But my family—what should I tell them? They will be worried and perhaps follow after us."

"Do not be concerned about that." He smiled, patting her hand. "I have a confederate within your family."

"Francesca?" Elizabeth asked with sudden insight.

"None other, and in the years to come we will always have her to thank for showing me the way to win your heart." He bent down and kissed her lightly on the lips. "For now, I think it best if we repair to supper. My coach will be waiting for you when it is time to leave; you will easily recognize it by the crest on the door. And do not worry about your family. Francesca has assured me she will manage everything."

Elizabeth could not eat a thing at supper, she was so excited, nor could she remember how she managed to get through the rest of the night. She was certain that everyone who glanced her way was guessing her secret, and it was all she could do to keep the news to herself. She even felt an inexplicable desire to tell Charlie of her planned flight, partly to keep her promise of the other day to let him know when she made her decision, and partly so that she might have someone to share her happiness with. But she wisely refrained from giving in to this impulse, and instead contented herself by exchanging several significant glances with Francesca.

When the time came for leavetaking, Elizabeth was fearful that she would not find Ivor's coach among the many others, or that her flight would be discovered before she could reach him. Then she saw him open the door and beckon her in, and she joined him gladly.

# EIGHT

Charles Buckley was at breakfast the next morning when his manservant handed him a message requesting his presence at Upper Grosvenor Street on a matter of some urgency. It was in an unfamiliar hand, and it took him some moments to decide that the single scrawled initial at the bottom of the missive was an F. He finished his breakfast rather more quickly than usual but without undue haste, wondering what Francesca wished to see him about with such dispatch at such an early hour.

He arrived at Upper Grosvenor Street in good time and was shown into the drawing room. Above his head he could hear several sets of footsteps crossing and recrossing the floor, and their insistent tap-tap-tap gave him his first sense of foreboding, his first inkling that all was not as it should be. Hearing his aunt shout "Nancy!" at the top of the stairs in a most uncharacteristic bellow convinced him that something was definitely amiss, and from there it took but a few short leaps of his imagination to suspect the worst. His uncle had fallen down the stairs and broken his neck! There was an outbreak of bubonic plague among the servants! Elizabeth! Something had happened to Elizabeth!

This last thought was the most distressing of all, and Charles had worked himself up into a fine state of agitation by the time his aunt flung open the door, regarded him gravely, and announced in tragic tones nothing more than what Charlie had expected to hear:

"Elizabeth has been abducted!"

By this time Charles would not have been surprised if she had announced that Napoleon himself had escaped from exile once more and was even now in the dining room taking tea. In fact, he was almost relieved, for abduction was at least a lesser evil than mutilation or death.

Before he was able to open his mouth and ask for details, Mrs. Locke cut him short,

"I cannot explain now. Francesca! Charles is here!" This was brayed in the general direction of upstairs, and then she turned back to Charles. "George has just gone round to hire a post chaise, and I am busy packing. Oh dear, oh dear, I do hope we will not be too late." She turned and went back up the stairs, muttering, "Oh dear, oh dear, oh dear," until Charles heard her shout, "Emma! Stop that sniffling and help me with this box!"

Francesca came to him a few minutes later, and finally Charles saw some hope of an explanation.

"I came as soon as I could," he said. "Your note did not explain—what is all this about Elizabeth's being abducted?"

Francesca threw her hands dramatically into the air. "It is too true. I am glad you were able to come so quickly. We are all making preparations to follow them, but we will not be ready to leave for at least an hour, and a post chaise is so slow. If you were to set out immediately on horseback I feel certain you would reach them all the sooner."

"Follow who? On horseback? I'm sorry, but I don't quite follow you," Charles exclaimed. "Do you mean to tell me that you know who it is who has abducted Lizzie?"

"Why, certainly! It is none other than Lord Westbridge!" Francesca draped herself on the settee in a tragic pose. "I have never trusted that man! To think

103

that he could do something like this! Elizabeth will be ruined!"

Charlie's anxiety was allayed somewhat when he heard Lord Westbridge's name mentioned, for he had been envisioning a band of ruffians numbering twenty at the least and all armed with assorted pistols, guns, and knives.

"I see," he said calmly, taking a seat near her. "Please tell me why you are so certain it is Westbridge. Have you received some message from him?"

"No, but who else could it be?" she asked him, then wailed, "And it is all my fault! I encouraged him! I actually said to him the other night—just in passing, you understand—that Elizabeth was of such a romantic turn of mind, just the sort of girl who longed to be swept off her feet and carried away! And now he has done it!"

"That is hardly substantial evidence," Charles persisted. "Have you nothing stronger on which to base your supposition?"

"I saw it with my own two eyes!" Francesca announced in thrilling tones.

"What?" Charlie leaped up. "You saw her being taken away and did nothing about it?"

"I did not know what I was seeing," Francesca admitted miserably. "We returned home in two carriages last night, and I assumed Elizabeth was in the other one. As my carriage drove away, I saw a figure being helped into Ivor's coach by two footmen—I recognized it by the crest on the door, of course. At the time I only thought it would be an interesting bit of gossip if I could learn who that lady was. Then this morning when we discovered that Elizabeth had not come home at all, I knew only too well the identity of that mysterious lady." She pulled a lace handkerchief out of her sleeve and dabbed her eyes with it.

Charles appeared strangely unmoved by this tale of woe. "But why do you say she was abducted?" he asked.

*"Madre de Dios!"* Francesca exclaimed, jumping up. "Did I not just tell you that I saw it with my own two

eyes?" Those same eyes were now blazing gloriously with indignation.

Charles cleared his throat. "What I mean to say is, perhaps she went willingly. I am not unaware that she has some feelings for Lord Westbridge, and although I am disappointed that she did not come to me first, as she promised, it does not surprise me greatly to hear she has run off with him."

This gave Francesca pause. "Are you then suggesting that they planned this elopement?" He nodded. "That they are even now on their way to Green Gage, or whatever that place is called?"

"Gretna Green."

"Thank you. You are seriously suggesting that Elizabeth went off to her wedding without so much as a clean pair of drawers?" Francesca's tone indicated only too well how ridiculous she found this notion to be.

Charles was slightly embarrassed by her intimate reference to undergarments, but allowed that was exactly what he was suggesting.

"You fool! You block! You stone!" Francesca burst out.

" 'You worse than senseless thing,' " Charlie prompted.

"I am glad you can find it all so amusing," Francesca said with biting irony. "And next you will tell me that you will not go after them."

"If they have eloped, that is their business. I have no illusions about Elizabeth's feelings for me." He shrugged slightly and turned away. "I do not wish to stand in the way of her happiness—even if that happiness does not lie with me."

"A very noble sentiment—and very English!" Francesca spat out with disgust. "If only you had some hot Spanish blood in you, this would not have happened in the first place. Even if she did go willingly—which I tell you she did not—it would be your own fault. When have you ever done anything more than merely kiss her hand, or compliment her on her dress? You are a worm, a slug, and now you will allow another man to have the woman you love!"

"It is precisely because I love her that I will let another man have her, if that is what will make her happy," Charles said quietly.

"You are the worst lizard that ever slunk across the face of the earth!" Francesca cried hotly, adding several more insults in Spanish. Then she stopped short, seeing that Charles was unmoved, and sighed. "But all this is getting us nowhere. Every moment you waste brings Elizabeth one moment closer to destruction and ruination." She stepped up behind him and placed a hand on his shoulder, and when she spoke again her tone was restrained, even gentle. "If Ivor wished to marry Elizabeth, what was to stop him from proposing at Emma's ball? How can I make you believe that his intentions are not honorable? How can I convince you that the girl I saw being handed into that coach last night required the aid of two strong footmen, each holding an arm?"

Charles turned around and regarded her seriously, for her reasoning tone had done more to convince him of the truth of what she said than a thousand insults would have done.

"You did not tell me that before," he said. "You are quite certain she was coerced?"

"I saw it with my own two eyes," she repeated. "What is more, I doubt very much that they are headed for Green Gage. It is much more likely that he has taken her to his home, Westham Park, where he can have his wicked way with her at his leisure."

"You believe he would be brazen enough to take her to his own home?" Charlie asked incredulously.

Francesca shrugged. "It is only a guess, but it is the best we have come up with." She saw that he was weakening and pressed her advantage. "It seems to me that your duty is plain, as plain as the fact that Elizabeth herself knew nothing of this *elopement,* as you have called it, else she surely would have kept her promise to let you know first. In any case, she would not have kept it a secret from *me;* she would be too excited by the plan to keep it completely to herself. No,

I tell you, she has been carried off against her will and to no good purpose!"

"I must go after her!" Charlie exclaimed, as if this were a totally novel idea.

Francesca breathed a sigh of relief. "Excellent!" she said. "You must try to reach them before the brute has violated my dear Elizabeth. I am not well acquainted with the geography of your country, but I have learned that Lord Westbridge's family home is in Northhamptonshire. Is that a very long journey?"

"A full day's journey by coach if they take the toll road north and make no stops," Charlie told her.

"Then you will easily catch up with them in time," Francesca said confidently. "They will certainly have to stop to change horses and have something to eat."

"But what if they are not to be found on that road? What if they have gone in some other direction entirely?"

"We will worry about that later, after we have looked in the most obvious place first. Go now. Take the fastest horse in my uncle's stable."

"I am not a very good rider," Charlie pointed out.

"Holy Mother of God, have mercy on my soul!" Francesca threw her hands up. "We left the ball at three this morning, it is now almost ten. They have seven hours' start on you—and you waste time telling me of your riding skill!"

"I will do the best I can," Charlie declared stoutly.

"That is all I ask," Francesca said. "We will follow in the post chaise as soon as we are ready. Go now."

Elizabeth was not yet ruined, at least not in the sense that Francesca meant, although both her gown and her temper were nearing that perilous state. She sat in what was euphemistically called a private parlor in this dingy little excuse for an inn, but was actually no more than a closet with a table in the center and very little room for servants to circumnavigate it as they served a meal. Her hair had fallen from its pins and the hem of her gown was bedraggled and brown from dirt. She was hot and sticky and hungry and had

107

long since come to realize that this whole escapade was a large mistake.

The adventure had begun comfortably enough. The escape itself had gone quite smoothly, and she was certain no one had seen her enter Ivor's coach. Once she was cozily situated against the cushions an exhilaration came over her like nothing she had ever experienced before. She was actually running away with the man she loved to become his bride! What a tale to tell her—and Ivor's—grandchildren. She had always felt she was destined for adventures of this kind—how wonderful to be proved right!

Her initial exhilaration did not last long, however. It was stuffy in the coach, but when Elizabeth requested that Ivor open a window, she was informed that the night air blowing in would be very bad for her health. Of course, this was couched in the most tender terms, with every consideration for her well-being, but Elizabeth could not help thinking that the heat in the coach was a great deal worse for her health than any amount of cool night air. She did not argue, though. She could not be so presumptuous as to gainsay this dashing soldier who had dared to sweep her away; nevertheless, the defeat rankled.

When the first rays of the rising sun were perceived through the window, Elizabeth thought she might in all conscience ask once more for the window to be raised, as it would no longer be night air blowing into the coach. But apparently her education had been most faulty in this regard, for it was pointed out to her, quite firmly, that it was not only night air that was unhealthy, but any blowing air at all.

"You see, my love," Ivor explained rationally, "I am subject to a pain in my neck whenever I am caught in a strong draft, and I should not like you to suffer from the same affliction."

Elizabeth reflected, unkindly, that it appeared she already did suffer from that affliction in a figurative sense, but again she did not argue. After all, he was only looking after her own best interests—he would make a most thoughtful, solicitous husband.

They traveled mostly in silence, each thinking of the consequences of this most important step they had taken. For her part, Elizabeth was wondering whether Francesca was right in supposing that Ivor's disregard of her opinion, even on matters as trivial as fresh air, could indeed be altered after they were married. Elizabeth was used to having her own way and did not like to be thwarted; but surely if Ivor loved her he would soon see that to bend, just a little, to her will would not reduce his dignity one whit.

Ivor was completely unaware of the seeds of discontent he had sown in his beloved. Instead, he was feeling rather pleased with himself that his duty was nearly done and he could soon return to his old habits, leaving Elizabeth in the country, where he would visit her periodically to ensure that his family grew regularly. And, of course, he would bring her to town for a few weeks during the season every year. The Westham family jewels would look remarkably well on her elegant neck, and he would like to be able to show them off every now and then. Yes, he decided, he had made a most acceptable choice, well worth the inconvenience of this precipitate journey.

It was nearing nine in the morning and Elizabeth's thoughts had been on breakfast for quite some time when disaster struck in the form of a young blood in a curricle, barreling down the road toward them and driving the coach off into a ditch. It was almost a relief for Elizabeth to be tumbled out of the door, for the cool morning air was most refreshing to her, and she was not hurt at all in the fall. Ivor immediately helped her to her feet and inquired after her health, and when he was satisfied that she had suffered no injury, he turned to shake a futile fist at the receding back of the curricle driver.

The coach was not upended, but its two left wheels were firmly implanted in a ditch, so that it leaned drunkenly to one side. After a few minutes' inspection, the coachman came up to Ivor and evaluated the damage.

"There's nothing broke, my lord, but we'll need some help pulling her out. To my recollection, my lord, there's an inn a mile or so up the road. Best we head for that and seek aid there."

"Very well," Ivor said, a distracted frown on his face. He turned to Elizabeth. "I cannot tell you how sorry I am, my love. This is not turning out at all the way I envisioned it."

Elizabeth's spirits had been quite restored by this delightful new episode in her adventure, which had been turning out to be quite dull until now. There was nothing like a little adversity to set one's blood circulating again! She replied cheerfully that she did not mind in the least, and took Ivor's arm so they could walk up the road together.

Her cheerfulness faded as "a mile or so" stretched into something like four miles, during which she had a terrible time trying to keep up with Ivor's long strides. She repeatedly asked him to slow down, and so he would for a minute or two, then, his mind elsewhere, his stride would lengthen again and Elizabeth would be left behind. He promised her that they would have a good meal when they finally reached the inn, and this thought sustained her, as did the case which the footman carried and which she hoped would contain a few items for her comfort, such as soap and perhaps even another gown. After all, Ivor had planned everything else with such care; there was no reason he should not have extended his thoughtfulness to her personal comfort.

In this she was mistaken. Hopes of a good meal were dashed when she finally laid eyes upon the Beak and Claw, which was hardly more than a dingy alehouse and appeared to attract business off the road only because of a dusty, ill-spelled placard stating that it was the "Last In before the Tolgate." The management was in no better repair than the building itself, and it was a very scruffy woman padding along on carpet slippers who showed Elizabeth into a tiny bedroom where she might freshen up, cringing obsequiously all the while, and whining how unused she was to doing for the gentry.

Elizabeth listened until the padding footsteps had died away before she went across the hallway and tapped at Ivor's door. He seemed genuinely surprised that she thought he might have packed a change of clothing for her.

"Why, it never occurred to me, my love," he told her. "Besides, where would I obtain a set of female garments?" He seemed mildly offended that she should expect him to have such items in his possession.

"You could have borrowed something from your sister," Elizabeth pointed out reasonably.

"And what would my sister have thought had I asked to borrow her clothing?" he asked with upraised eyebrows.

"I think you should have made some provision for me, just the same!" she exclaimed. "You must have known that I would be wearing a ball gown, it should have occurred to you that I might have needed something else. I notice you packed enough for yourself!" This was quite true, for as she looked past him into the room she saw his footman shaking out clean linen and trousers for him.

"Elizabeth, my love, there is no need to raise your voice," he said, lowering his own accordingly. "I had no idea we would be stopping before we reached Westham Park, where of course you will find everything possible for your comfort. Now you run along and wash up and then we will have a nice breakfast."

Elizabeth did not like being spoken to like a recalcitrant child, but as there was nothing else to do, she obeyed him. The "nice breakfast" turned out to be greasy eggs and dried-up ham, with half a meat pie that was a bit green around the edges. As soon as Mrs. Carpet Slippers had served them and scuffed away, Elizabeth declared:

"This food isn't fit for a dog!"

111

Ivor had already tucked into his breakfast and looked up with surprise. "What is wrong with it?"

"How can you ask?" Elizabeth said, horrified at his insensitivity. "I am sure these eggs were not fresh, and as for the ham, it must be three years old."

"It tastes fine to me," Ivor said. "My love, if you had starved on the Peninsula, as I did, you would not complain about this meal, I can assure you."

"Well, I did not starve on the Peninsula, thank you very much, but it does appear I will starve here," Elizabeth said tartly. "But I don't see that is anything to the point. The point is, I have been served with inedible food and I would like very much for you to do something about it." She folded her arms and glared at him, determined not to be coddled out of this dispute.

Ivor reluctantly put down his knife and fork. "Very well, my love, I will see if there is anything else to be had."

A few minutes later he returned, shaking his head. "She says she has nothing else. She can kill a chicken for us, but that will take several hours to prepare."

"Well, I hope you told her to go ahead and do it," Elizabeth said.

"Why, no, I didn't," he replied, surprised. "Surely we will be gone in several hours more."

"For heaven's sake, Ivor, it will take that long at least for the coach to be hauled out. Did you not think we would want some lunch before we left?"

"I had thought this breakfast to be ample," he said, taking his place again. "I suggest you follow my example and eat what is in front of you."

"*I'll* see to it then!" she exclaimed, arising so suddenly that her chair fell back against the wall with a clatter.

When she returned she appeared to be in a slightly better temper. "Honestly, Ivor, it occurs to me that you are quite helpless in some matters. There is an entire village just over the hill, past the tollgate, and there is another inn there, which must be better than this one, for it certainly could not be worse. It is but five minutes' walk, and pedestrians do not have to pay at the gate."

"But we cannot leave here," Ivor protested. "I told Robert we would wait for him."

"Even if he did drive us off the road, he cannot be so stupid that he would not understand a message left for him that told him to look for us at the next inn."

"My coachman is not stupid," Ivor said doggedly, "and we will remain here."

"That is lovely," Elizabeth said with great irony. "Not only am I to starve to death, but I must wallow in filth as well."

"There is food before you," Ivor pointed out.

"Filth!" Elizabeth exclaimed, scattering a handful of the eggs across the table for emphasis. "You sit there, eating that slop, and paying no attention to me whatsoever. I say we are going to the other inn."

"I can hardly *not* pay attention to you, you are speaking so loudly." He wiped his mouth with his pocket handkerchief, as no napkins had been provided. "In fact, I think this whole village you speak of must be paying attention to you. I never imagined that you had such a temper, Elizabeth, and I must admit it is not a happy discovery."

"It is only aroused when I am treated with great injustice," she declared.

"I hardly see how it is *my* fault we were pushed off the road. It is not as if we had lost a wheel or anything else as a result of carelessness—I checked everything most thoroughly before we left."

"And as thorough as you were, it did not occur to you to pack a change of clothing for me?"

"Are we back to that again?" he said with a sigh. "You have made me lose whatever appetite I may have had. Very well, Elizabeth, I will walk to this village and if this other inn you have heard about is better than this one, I will return for you and we will remove there, leaving a message for Robert, who, I am sure, is perfectly capable of understanding it."

113

"Thank you," Elizabeth said with little grace, as he left her to stew alone.

While she waited for him she reflected that perhaps she could have held her temper better. It was not an auspicious way to begin a marriage, to rail out at her bridegroom like a common fishwife. She gave a great yawn and remembered that she had not slept the night before, and that this might be a factor in her ill temper. She resolved that she would not be angry with Ivor any longer. After all, it was true that none of this was his fault, and he had walked into town to seek out a better place for her. But however charitable she planned to be, something was lost from the adventure that would not be regained. The excitement was gone, and she mourned its passing with some regret.

The second inn was indeed better than the first, Ivor reported back to her a few minutes later, and they removed there speedily. Elizabeth was finally able to have a neat, clean chamber where she was provided with the soap and hot water she so longed for and even a plain but clean gown belonging to the innkeeper's daughter, Molly.

When she came downstairs for lunch, Ivor informed her that the coach had sunk even deeper in the mire and it looked as though they would not be leaving before the evening. "That is, if you do not mind traveling all night," he said with extreme politeness.

"I do not mind. If I cannot have the window open, at least it will be more comfortable to travel at a time when the sun is not beating in."

She could have bitten her tongue off as soon as she said this, for she saw Ivor stiffen as he replied coldly, "Undoubtedly." She tried desperately to think of a way to make amends as they ate their lunch in silence, punctuated only by scrupulously polite requests for the salt to be passed.

When she had finished, she leaned back and smiled at him broadly. "I feel ever so much better now," she said. "All I wanted was a good meal. Now perhaps I will take a nap and then I will be fully restored."

Ivor did not reply.

Elizabeth leaned over the table toward him, smiled winningly, and said, "Pax?"

He regarded her coldly. "I beg your pardon?"

"Can we not make peace? I apologize for my show of temper and would like to forget all about it now." She felt she was being more than generous and that he would certainly soften now.

"Indeed?" he said. "Unfortunately, I cannot forget so easily. It was a very great shock to me to see you fling things about and rail on so."

Elizabeth wondered what he meant until she remembered the eggs. She gave a slight grunt of exasperation. "Honestly, Ivor, I would hardly call brushing a few eggs onto the table 'flinging things about.'"

"That is where we differ, for I certainly do," he maintained. "And I find it to be a most unfortunate tendency. I am surprised at you, Elizabeth."

"I am surprised at you!" she cried. "Why can we not just forget the whole thing? I have forgiven you."

He raised his eyebrows. "Forgiven me for what? *I* have done nothing reprehensible."

Elizabeth's temper rose and she stood up in preparation for throwing the mustard pot at his head and showing him the true meaning of "flinging things about." But before she could carry out her dastardly plan, Charles Buckley entered the room.

When Elizabeth threw herself into his arms and exclaimed, "Charlie! I am so glad to see you!" Charles needed no further confirmation of Francesca's allegations of abduction.

He glowered at his rival over Elizabeth's shoulder and said, "Look here, Westbridge, I think you have some explaining to do."

# NINE

Richard Tanner was clearly a gentleman. That much was obvious, despite the fact that he rode into town alone, with no more baggage that what his horse could carry behind the saddle. But that horse was a fine one, a high-stepper whose noble bloodlines were apparent even through the light covering of dust that had accumulated on the journey. Neither could the dust disguise the expensive cut of Mr. Tanner's coat, nor that his boots were of the finest leather and very nearly new.

As he mounted the hillock that hid the little town of Budgate to the south, Mr. Tanner breathed a sigh of relief that his journey for the day was nearly ended. He looked forward to a light supper and a pleasant night's rest at the George, where he always broke his journey when he traveled from his home in the north back to London or Oxford. Of course, if he continued to ride, pressing his mount slightly, he could reach London before nightfall, especially at this time of year, when the sun did not set until after nine o'clock, but he had long ago taken a liking to this sleepy little village and an even greater liking to Mr. Currier's cellar, which boasted a variety of wines seldom to be found outside the larger metropolitan centers.

As he attained the crest of the hill, he paused to wipe

the dust out of his eyes and wondered momentarily if he had mistaken his way. For the sight that greeted him was not at all like that sleepy little village he had been expecting. It seemed as though everyone in the town was milling about on the high street, and he was certain he saw Daniel Currier himself, of the famous cellar, performing some sort of mystical ceremony with other high-standing members of the community. As Mr. Tanner drew nearer, he could see more plainly that they were measuring out the ground and planting stakes, smack in the middle of the market square, for what purpose he knew not but proposed to find out quickly.

The George was at the far end of the high street, and it took Mr. Tanner quite some time to navigate through the milling crowd. When he reached the innyard he was relieved to see another familiar face and know indeed that he was in Budgate. Jemmy Breadlow, the inn's drawer and the intended of Molly Currier, was seated at a table in the yard making entries in a ledger as a long line of men filed past him.

"Ho! Jemmy!" Mr. Tanner cried, and the young man looked up.

"Mr. Tanner!" He grinned. "Molly's got your room ready inside. If you'll leave the horse in the back, I'll see to him later."

"But what is going on?" Mr. Tanner called back to him, over the heads of a crowd that snickered and laughed at his ignorance.

"Why, there's to be a fight in the market square!" Jemmy called back cheerfully. "Would you care to make a wager?" He dipped his pen in the pot of ink before him and held it expectantly over the ledger.

"No, no." Mr. Tanner laughed. "I do not even know who is fighting."

"The smart money's going on his lordship," a man in the queue informed him.

Mr. Tanner was about to ask Jemmy the names of the principals, but that enterprising soul had turned

117

back to his bookmaking. Mr. Tanner shrugged and smiled and led his horse around back to the stableyard. As it appeared likely that it would be some time before Jemmy would have a chance to look after his horse, Mr. Tanner saw to what was necessary himself. Then, taking his saddlebag, he entered the inn through the back door, which led to the taproom.

This was nearly full of townsfolk and nearby farmers who had ridden over as soon as they heard of the intended fight, and Molly Currier was behind the bar doing a brisk business.

Mr. Tanner was accosted as soon as he entered.

"Here's a likely-looking gentleman," someone said from a table in the corner. "Hey there, sir, want to put some money on the fight? I've got five bob says his lordship will win."

"Whist, Bobby, and what do you know of it? I say the little blond chap will break him down in five minutes."

"Let's see the color of yer money, then!"

Mr. Tanner approached the bar.

"There hasn't been a fight like this since the Great Jew Mendoza himself fought it out with our tollkeeper," he was informed by a friendly young man.

"What do *you* know about *that,* Sam? You couldn't have been more than five at the time," his pal said derisively.

"Me dad told me of it! He was there. Hey, Dad," he shouted across the room. "Tell Bill Bodkins here about Mendoza's fight!"

"Now there was a spectacle," Sam's dad said expansively to the room at large, and went on to describe the bout, which had lasted no more than twenty minutes, twenty years ago. It appeared it would take much longer than that to retell it, especially with all the corrections and corroborations from others who had been present.

Mr. Tanner finally succeeded in drawing Molly's attention, and after she had acknowledged him she turned to one of her other customers.

"Here, you, Dave Watkins, look after the tap for me, and mind you don't drink away all our profits."

She removed her apron and handed it to Dave Watkins, who took it and held it at arm's length with a comical look at his cronies, some of whom laughed and one of whom said, "Just like home, eh, Davey?"

"Oh, Mr. Tanner, I am so sorry you should find us in such confusion," Molly said when they had made their way out of the taproom. "I'm sure *I* don't remember when such a thing has happened before. But your room is ready, if you'll follow me, and a good thing you wrote ahead or I might have given it to his lordship or the young lady or the other young gentleman. Me dad told me to, in fact, but no, I told him, Mr. Tanner comes here regular and deserves better treatment than a very suspicious-appearing couple what arrives on foot, even if he is a duke and who cares for such things anyway, I told him. Dad's a republican at heart, you know, and that persuaded him, I can tell you."

As she spoke she led Mr. Tanner to the room he usually occupied when he stopped here. He placed his saddlebag on the bed as Molly opened the window to air the room out.

"I'd send Cissy up with some hot water, but I fear she's gone out to watch the proceedings. The girl is never where you want her to be. And dinner will be a bit late, I'm afraid—me mum's all alone in the kitchen—but I can serve you some tea now, if you like."

Mr. Tanner said that would be fine, and Molly appeared ready to leave him, but he stopped her.

"Molly, do you have a minute to tell me what this is all about?" he asked.

She smiled and said, "I suppose so. Dave Watkins is trustworthy enough and I'm that worn out I could do with a bit of a sit-down."

"Then pray sit down and tell me all about it," he invited.

"Don't mind if I do," she said, and with a large sigh placed herself in a chair. She was a comely girl of about

119

eighteen, with a cheerful countenance. Although her hair had begun to come loose from its pins, this gave an appearance more attractive than messy, and her clean white tucker was a truer indication of her usual tidy appearance.

"Well, it started around lunchtime when his lordship arrived with a young lady." She sniffed. "And wasn't it I who had to give her the loan of my best dress? For all her fine airs she was as bedraggled as a wet hen and that put out with his lordship, you could see in a minute." She said "his lordship" in a faintly derogatory way. "I put them in the best parlor, of course—they'd been taken in by that sign at the Beak and Claw and served up with one of Mrs. Needham's greasy delicacies, so as you can imagine, their appetite was good. And then I thought no more about them until an hour later when this other gentleman arrived, asking if such a couple was here. He had passed their coach stuck in a ditch some miles back."

She grinned as she related this next part of her tale. "He was a young, blond gentleman, and seemed to know what he was about, so I showed him to the parlor, but I didn't quite close the door all the way—we've so little entertainment in Budgate, you know," she added by way of apology, although she did not seem at all ashamed of her eavesdropping.

Next she had beckoned Jemmy over, to be entertained with her, and their curiosity was well rewarded.

There was quite a smashing argument between the two gentlemen, with the lady putting in a word now and again, to the effect that she wished to return home and hoped never to see his lordship again as long as she lived. His lordship seemed quite agreeable to this proposition, declaring that the lady was a fishwife and not his idea of what a lady should be at all. At this, the lady very naturally burst into tears. The other gentleman said that he was very glad his lordship felt that way, for he planned to take the lady home immediately and would not hesitate to tell the world of his lordship's despicable behavior.

His lordship took exception to that, declaring that his intentions toward the lady had been honorable and producing a license to prove it. Then he said he would not rest until the other gentleman had given him satisfaction, for he had impeded his honor.

"Impeded his honor?" Mr. Tanner interrupted.

"P'raps that is not the right word," Molly admitted. "His lordship used a great many words I didn't understand, and I am not at all sure they were all quite proper, although the lady didn't seem to object."

"Quite," Mr. Tanner said dryly, enjoying the tale immensely. "You had come to the part where the blond gentleman impugned his lordship's honor."

"That's the very word!" Molly declared, pleased. "You are so very clever, Mr. Tanner." Then she continued.

It seemed that the blond gentleman thought his lordship was joking, and the more he thought that, the angrier his lordship became.

"And then the lady *did* object to their language, I can tell you." Molly laughed. "Jemmy almost sent me away, but I gave him a right kick and that kept him in his place."

Evidently, the lady had objected not only to the language, but to the very notion that the two should fight a duel at all, and now she became just as angry at the blond gentleman as she had been with his lordship, telling him that he should not have come after them at all, for she and his lordship were to be married.

"But the lady couldn't seem to make up her mind, for the next thing she said was all she wanted was to go home and change into some decent clothes—and this wearing my best dress," Molly footnoted indignantly. "Then his lordship went on at length about how *her* honor as well as his own had been impeded, until she said, very crossly, 'Oh, very well. Charlie, you may as well fight a duel with him or we shall have no peace at all. But don't blame *me* when one of you is killed.'

"She didn't seem too concerned about it, if you ask me," Molly continued, "but then I suppose she didn't

121

think they wouldn't really carry it through, especially when this Charlie pointed out that he had no skill with swords or pistols, and his lordship laughed at him in a very nasty way and said what should they do in that case, resort to fisticuffs?"

Apparently the blond gentleman had thought this an excellent idea, and as they had both been trained by someone named Jackson, they were both well acquainted with the sport and all its rules.

"Jemmy seemed to set great store by this man Jackson, though I don't know why," Molly said. "But he was most anxious to help arrange the fight. He and the two gentlemen walked up to the market square, to see where they could set the ring. Jemmy fetched his friend Dooby Cratchit, who is a great follower of the fancy, as they called it, to see that it would all be done proper. Then, of course, as soon as the news got around that there was to be a fight everyone came out to take a look at the two gentlemen and size them up so they would know where to put their money. In a town such as this, news travels fast, and now it seems everyone has dropped whatever he was doing for gainful employment to come out and watch two grown men behave like silly children." She stood up. "And speaking of gainful employment—I must return to my duties. Dave Watkins has most likely given half the town free beer by now."

Mr. Tanner had become very thoughtful during the last part of her narrative, and now asked her to describe for him the blond gentleman, the one called Charlie.

"Why, he's a nice-enough-looking gentleman, although he wears spectacles and is not very tall." She grinned. "I've placed five bob on him myself—I liked the way he smiled at me."

"He is not called Mr. Buckley, is he?" Mr. Tanner asked her.

"Why, yes, now that you mention it, I believe that is the name he gave."

"Where is he? You must take me to him at once!"

122

"You will have to go looking for him, Mr. Tanner. After the three of them had their tea—and it wasn't a very peaceful meal, as you can imagine—the blond gentleman went out for a walk. The others are resting in their rooms if you would like to see either of them."

"No, it is Mr. Buckley I must see. He is a great friend of mine!"

Molly was much pleased by this news, especially since she had already put her money on Mr. Tanner's friend, and promised she would tell him as soon as Mr. Buckley returned to the inn. In the meantime, she would serve his tea in his room, and Mr. Tanner had to be satisfied with this for the moment.

At first Elizabeth had considered the idea of two grown men resorting to fisticuffs, like so many schoolboys, completely ridiculous and argued strenuously against it. But her hope that she could make both men see reason and go quietly home was futile, even when she continued the argument over tea, refreshed and revitalized by a brief nap.

"There are bigger things at stake here than you can conceive of, my dear Elizabeth," Ivor told her condescendingly. "When a man's honor is impugned"—Elizabeth was growing heartily sick of this expression—"it is only natural that he should wish to restore it. Of course, I would not expect you to understand such a thing, Elizabeth. Women are not brought up to follow such a rigid code of honor as men are; indeed, with their weaker natures, it is too much to expect them to follow such a noble ideal."

Elizabeth objected to this statement, pointing out that women are taught from an early age that their honor is the only thing of value they have to offer a husband.

Ivor hid a smile and said kindly, "We are not speaking of chastity, my dear, but of honor. They are not quite the same thing."

Elizabeth controlled the urge she felt to hurl the
123

remaining tea cakes in his face, and said instead, "But why must you settle your dispute in such a bloody manner? Surely the laws against dueling were passed with good reason?"

"By middle-class merchants who have as little notion of honor as you do, my dear," Ivor said with feeling. "But as it happens, Mr. Buckley and I will be doing nothing illegal when we meet in the ring."

"Perhaps that is why Elizabeth objects," Charles said mildly. "After all, fisticuffs do not have quite the air of respectability as fighting with swords or pistols would have. There is something decidedly plebeian about two men fighting it out with their bare fists."

Elizabeth reddened, for she had indeed been thinking something of the kind. She was ashamed to mention her other fear, though, which was that Charles was hopelessly outclassed. She did not see how he could come out the victor in any battle with Westbridge, whether it was fought with fists, swords, pistols, or any other weapon men had devised to inflict injury on one another. Of course, there was something flattering about the whole idea of two men fighting over her, and it *would* have been nice if they had chosen a more conventional, although illegal, means of settling their dispute. But then there would have been the possibility of Charlie's being fatally injured, instead of just grievously injured.

Ivor had thought Charlie's remark was addressed to him and had begun expounding upon the history of dueling and fisticuffs respectively, explaining in a pedantic manner that there was as much science in using one's fists correctly as in using the blade. He had forgotten all about his original objection to meeting Charles in the ring, and now spoke as if the whole thing had been his own idea.

Elizabeth interrupted him, just as he had started an important digression on the benefits of sparring saloons on the physical health of the upper classes, by rising abruptly and saying in a cross voice, "As there are still

124

some hours before this travesty is to take place, I believe I will attempt to get some more rest. It is obvious neither of you has any regard at all for my feelings in the matter."

She left the two gentlemen alone, and as they had nothing much to say to one another, they soon went their separate ways, Ivor to follow Elizabeth's example, and Charles to wander about the town, wondering exactly how he had gotten himself into this situation.

Charles would not have told Westbridge as much, but secretly he agreed with Elizabeth that it was ridiculous for men to settle their differences on a field of battle. He would have been content simply to take Elizabeth home with him, agreeing with Westbridge to forget the whole thing. Indeed, he could not remember to save his life how he had "impugned" the older man's honor, though he must have done so, for the phrase kept cropping up. He supposed it had something to do with the fact that he had thought Westbridge's intentions dishonorable until he had been shown the special license that man carried in his pocketbook. Nonetheless, Charles wondered if honor could be impugned in private. After all, honor itself was rather a public thing, depending upon the opinions of society at large. But who could bespeak a man's conscience? Doubtless there were many men who gave the outward show of honorableness, but deep inside were immoral blackguards, and vice versa.

Deep in these philosophical meanderings, Charles was surprised to note that quite a crowd had gathered already in the high street to witness the sporting event. As he wandered up to the market square he was accosted by Currier, the innkeeper, and invited to inspect the ring.

"Dooby Cratchit—he's the man," Currier explained to Charles. "A great follower of the fancy is he, and possessed of an official rule book from which we are taking the measurements. And," he added importantly, "those of us who is to judge have been making a

125

study of the rules so there shouldn't be any funny business—not that we would expect any, both of you being fine gentlemen, as you are."

"Of course," Charles answered gravely. "A very fine job Dooby has made of it, too."

"He's to be the ref," Currier told him. "He insisted. By the by, Mr. Buckley, Jemmy Breadlow, who's to marry my Molly, is taking bets in front of the inn, if you'd care to put any money down on yerself."

"Certainly not, Mr. Currier," Charles said with dignity. "A gentleman never wagers upon himself." He was not quite certain if this was true in fisticuffs, for certainly it was not true with horses, but it had a noble ring to it and would save his pocketbook.

"I didn't mean no offense, sir," Currier said hastily.

"No offense was taken," Charlie said kindly, then in a confidential voice, "How are the odds running, Mr. Currier?"

"I'll tell you, Mr. Buckley. They're running against you, that's a fact, but"—he held up a finger—"them that know something, like Dooby Cratchit, have put every penny on you, so there you have it!"

Charlie smiled and thanked him and watched for a moment as the men set the stakes on which to fasten the ropes, easily picking out the expert Dooby, who was giving orders in a very confident manner.

So the odds were against him, Charlie thought as he wandered off. Well, that was only to be expected. Westbridge was a larger man than he and naturally would be favored. Actually, it made little difference to him whether he won or lost, except for the illogical desire to prove himself to Elizabeth. And why should that matter to him any more? he thought with a trace of bitterness. She had clearly indicated her preference by running off with Westbridge, and if he had not been stupid enough to listen to Francesca, the two of them would be in Northhamptonshire now, standing before the local vicar.

Or maybe not. Charlie could not help but smile when

126

he remembered how genuinely glad Elizabeth had
been to see him, and the appealing way she had thrown
herself into his arms. He had then heard the whole
story of her disagreements with Westbridge from her
and had been hard pressed not to laugh aloud in front
of his lordship. Apparently, the man, for all his experience on the Peninsula, which he was so fond of bringing
up, did not know how to handle a normal English
woman or how to win an argument without appearing
to do so. He did not know when to mollify, or when to
finish an argument with a joke so that it might all
come to nothing. He expected women to be like his
ideal of them—seen and not heard, compliant in all
things. Yet he had chosen a woman who was completely opposite to that ideal, on appearances alone it
seemed, and when he learned that there was a real
person beneath the beautiful exterior, a real woman
who grew dirty and uncomfortable and hungry and
cross, he did not know how to handle her.

When Charlie thought of the condescending way
Westbridge spoke to Elizabeth, he wanted nothing so
much as to wipe the self-satisfied smirk off his face
with a good, strong left hook. Perhaps this was the real
reason he was fighting the man; not for any high-flown
ideals about Honor, but for the pure animal satisfaction of punching him until he was silly. Lizzie was
right, Charlie thought with a smile, he was nothing
more than an overgrown schoolboy, but somehow he
felt much better about himself knowing that he would
not do battle under false pretenses.

When he returned to the inn he heard his name
called out by a familiar voice.

"Charlie! Where have you been? I have been looking
all over for you!"

"Dick!" Charlie called happily upon recognizing his
friend. "What on earth are you doing here?"

"I always stay here on my way to London. Currier
here keeps a fine cellar." The two men shook hands and
slapped each other on the shoulder.

127

"Now what is all this about a fight?" Richard Tanner demanded. "It is lucky I arrived, or who would you have as your second?"

"Why, I never gave it a second thought," Charles said with a grin, allowing Richard time for an appreciative groan. "But now that you are here, I have nothing to worry about."

"Only this fellow you are to fight." His friend laughed. "I always knew you would come to no good when you left my fine tutelage at Oxford! Come, let us join your public in the taproom and you can tell me all the details over a pint of ale."

# TEN

The afternoon sun was still high in the sky as the two principals took their places in opposite corners of the ring. Indeed, if the fight should last so long, it would shine on them until half past nine. Charles Buckley thought that was more than enough time to whip some sense into his opponent, or as Richard Tanner pointed out when he heard this remark, to whip the sense out of him.

"For indeed, is not the insensibility of at least one of you the major object of this sporting event?" he asked, as Charles handed him his coat and he draped it neatly over the back of the chair that had been provided for the second's comfort. Diagonally across from them, Robert, the coachman, was performing the same service for Westbridge as he, too, stripped to his shirtsleeves.

Dooby Cratchit was still coaching the judges on the rules of the sport, and these three men, stalwart citizens of Budgate all, looked very solemn and serious in their seats on the sideline. Opposite them, Elizabeth had been given a place of honor, attended by Molly Currier. Her appearance had given rise to a great deal of whispering as new, improved versions of the reason for the bout were passed through the crowd. Not a few evil-minded souls craned their necks eagerly to see if her rumored condition showed itself in her figure yet, and matrons clicked disapprovingly and shielded younger daughters' ears from the tales that fell readily from everyone's lips. Even Mrs. Needham of the Beak and Claw had shuffled over to view the spectacle, starting a few rumors of her own about the extraordinary bad temper of the young lady and how she was so highborn she could not even eat ordinary food.

Jemmy Breadlow circulated through the crowd, taking the bets of those who had not seen the principals when they were examining the site earlier this afternoon. Opinion was divided on whether the money should be placed on his lordship's greater height and longer reach, or Young Blondie's more stocky evidence of strength and youthful vitality. Jemmy rather encouraged the former, for on the advice of Dooby Cratchit he had placed all of his money on Young Blondie and wished to keep the odds long, in hopes that his wedding day would no longer be delayed when he reaped his profits.

Dooby Cratchit was not the only one impressed by Charlie's muscular appearance in his shirtsleeves. Elizabeth was quite surprised when she realized that Ivor's broad shoulders, which she had so often admired, were largely the work of his tailor, while Charles had needed no padding in his coat to present a fashionably fit figure. In fact, when she heard Molly's murmured "Oh my, but he's a fine, strapping lad," Elizabeth felt a surge of pride, almost as though she herself were responsible for keeping Charlie's figure in trim.

The two gentlemen were now ready and approached the center of the ring, where they shook hands and listened to Dooby recite the list of rules, ending with the warning that one of the judges was the assistant magistrate and wouldn't hold with no shenanigans.

Then Dooby stepped back and lowered his arms, and the fight began.

At first the two men merely circled around, each throwing out a feint now and then which was not intended to meet its mark but to discover the quickness of the other. They were sizing each other up, looking each other over, each trying to determine his best strategy, but the crowd would not stand for this long and began shouting for some real fighting, and gradually the men closed in.

In these early minutes, Westbridge had the clear advantage with his longer reach. Charlie would have to move in a great deal closer than he really cared to if he ever hoped to land a punch, and would have to aim his jabs upward if he wished to hit Westbridge in any more vulnerable spot than his upper chest. But Charlie was quick at dodging the punches of the older man, and received only a few blows to the shoulders until Westbridge threw a lucky shot and drew first blood.

Elizabeth gasped and cried out for them to stop, but she was quickly hushed by those around her and regarded unsympathetically by Molly, until that girl paused to consider how she would feel if it were Jemmy who was in the ring.

Time was called and Charles returned to his corner, where Dick Tanner handed him a towel to wipe the blood from his nose and poured some cooling water over his head. He gave Charlie a questioning glance, and Charlie grinned in reply.

"Don't worry, Dick—it's all strategy. My nose bleeds if you so much as look at it cross-eyed, and it always gives the other fellow a false confidence. Always worked like a charm at Eton."

"Westbridge is no schoolboy," Dick pointed out.

"No, or he might be a better fighter," Charlie said with a laugh after he took a deep drink of water.

The two men returned to center ring, and now the fight began in earnest. Soon they were both drenched with sweat, and might as well not have been wearing shirts at all for all those garments concealed. More money had been placed on Westbridge during the time-out, and the cheering for him grew in volume as he found his rhythm, delivering blow after blow while keeping his opponent at arm's length so he could not reach him with a blow of his own. Several times Charlie almost went down, and each time Elizabeth's heart gave a sickening lurch until she saw him recover immediately, apparently unhurt.

A second time-out was called, but now Jemmy would accept no more bets, for he could not cover any more money placed on his lordship. Westbridge himself seemed confident that victory would soon be his as he bowed to the crowd, receiving their cheers graciously.

The fight resumed in much the same style, with Charles unable to move in close enough to deliver a punch of his own before Westbridge landed one first. Then Charles took what appeared to be a fearful wallop just below the ribcage, and as he doubled over Westbridge moved in for the kill.

But as soon as Westbridge was close enough, Charlie let forth with a volley of neatly timed jabs, ending with an uppercut to the jaw that sent Westbridge reeling. Charlie straightened up with a grin, and the crowd gave a roar of appreciation for his strategy that had worked so well.

Charlie did not give Westbridge time to recover from this staggering blow, but moved in on him once more, maneuvering around so that Westbridge was always facing west, with the setting sun in his eyes. Now the older man appeared to be tiring, and his punches began to fall too high, many of them going right over Charlie's shoulders. Charlie, on the other hand, seemed to gain new strength from every blow that met its mark. The mark Charlie seemed to be aiming for was the taller man's upper shoulders, until it became apparent to the spectators that it was his object to wear his opponent down until he could cut through his defenses and land a few more telling uppercuts to the jaw and face.

And Westbridge was playing right into his hands, allowing Charles to come as close as he pleased instead of working on his own advantage of his longer reach, as he had done before. The truth was, Ivor had never

132

engaged in a real fistfight before. Well versed with the science of fisticuffs he was, as any gentleman who frequented Gentleman Jackson's with any regularity was bound to be, but he now learned to his grief that sparring in a friendly fashion with protective gloves was a far cry from a barefisted fight with someone who was actually anxious to beat him to a pulp.

This stage of the fight lasted some time, for although Westbridge was taking a great deal of punishment, he was physically fit and probably could stand even more. Dooby Cratchit called several more time-outs, after each of which Westbridge returned refreshed and stronger, but each time his newfound strength waned more quickly until he reached a point where he could hardly throw out a blow of his own, but only stand there taking all that Charlie had to give. His face was now hardly recognizable as his own, for all the blood that had been drawn. He was brought to his knees several times, but managed to stagger back to his feet while Charlie waited for the count, dancing around and waving to the crowd, whose cheers were now all for him.

Then came a punch after which Westbridge could not even see his opponent for the shooting stars that crowded his vision, and as he lay on the ground, staring up at the sky, which seemed to be full of fireworks, he thought in a detached manner that this was a very comfortable position to be in, nor could he remember any pressing reason to rise again.

A great cheer went up from the crowd, and Charlie waved his arms happily and walked over to help Westbridge up and shake his hand. But for the first time since the fight had begun, Charlie misjudged Westbridge's height; he tripped on one outstretched leg and went down with a fearful crack, lying quite as still as the defeated man.

At first the crowd laughed good-naturedly, thinking it some kind of prank on his part, but when Elizabeth, who was close enough to see that it was indeed no prank, rushed to his side, the cheering changed to gasps of alarms and calls for the doctor.

"Charlie, oh my poor love, Charlie," Elizabeth murmured as she tried to revive him and failed. Dick Tanner entered the ring and poured a bucket of water on his head to no avail, and without thinking, in front of all the multitudes, Elizabeth removed her petticoat and used it as a pillow for Charlie's head until the doctor could determine if it was safe to move him.

"And furthermore, Elizabeth, if you wished to marry Lord Westbridge you certainly needn't have run off with him. I have no doubt that your father would have given his approval for the match and you could have been married quite conventionally from Upper Grosvenor Street and saved us all a great deal of trouble."

"Yes, Aunt Annabel, you are quite right," Elizabeth replied automatically, her attention divided between listening to Mrs. Locke's upbraiding and watching for the doctor to come downstairs with news of Charlie's condition.

The family had arrived just in time to see Charles carried into the inn on a gate, and as everyone seemed to be at sixes and sevens, Mrs. Locke lost no time in arranging everything to her liking. She immediately found an ally in Mrs. Currier, who didn't hold with fisticuffs and had disapproved silently of the whole business from the start. She did hold with running an efficient establishment, however, and while it was rare that she had so many guests at one time, and all of them quality, with Mrs. Locke's cooperation satisfactory accommodations were found for all and a meal was put into preparation for these late-arriving travelers who had not dined on the way.

These practical considerations out of the way, Mrs. Locke saw to the proper distribution of the family itself. Emma was sent to lie down upon her bed until dinner was ready, for she had moaned and sniffled during the entire journey on account of missing her evening at Almack's and consequently missing an opportunity to see Mr. Foxmoor, who would now forget her very existence and fix his attentions on some other female. Being told she was a silly girl did not help her disposition much, but seeing her safely out of the way for the moment helped her mother's disposition enormously.

Next, the two lady's maids, Francesca's Conchita and the Lockes' Harrigan, were given employment helping Molly make up the extra beds and helping Mrs. Currier prepare dinner, respectively. Mr. Locke's man, who could never be ordered about, sought out his master's bedroom on his own to do whatever it was that he did to increase his master's comfort, until such time as Conchita was finished with her duties, when he would seek her out to continue their flirtation, which had begun some weeks before.

Next, Elizabeth was pushed out of Charlie's bedroom, where it was most improper for her to be now that the doctor had begun his examination, and sent down to the private dining room, where her uncle began the lecture that her aunt completed after she had seen Francesca properly introduced to Mr. Tanner and entertaining him in the common room.

"Have you nothing to say for yourself, young lady?" Mrs. Locke asked her niece. Such sternness was out of character for her, and she could feel the strain it gave her heart, but she knew it was her duty as Elizabeth's guardian to make this effort. Elizabeth shook her lowered head, and Mrs. Locke turned to her husband with a sigh. "George, you talk to the girl."

Mr. Locke looked up from his newspaper. "What? Oh, yes, of course." He cleared his throat. "And what do you suppose your father would say to all of this?"

Elizabeth gave a glimmer of a smile. "Oh, I expect he will laugh and say it is just like me. He will be much more worried about poor Charlie. Auntie, mayn't I go up and see him now? The doctor has been such a long time."

"Very well," her aunt conceded, gratified to see by this expression of concern that her niece had at least a

135

few delicate sensibilities left after her adventures. "I will accompany you," she added, feeling that would satisfy both the proprieties and her own curiosity about the health of her nephew.

Elizabeth had quite forgotten that the doctor had another patient to see to, but was relieved to learn he had not been attending only Charles all this time. When she and her aunt arrived at the top of the stairs they discovered him coming out of Lord Westbridge's room.

"How is he, doctor?" Elizabeth asked.

"His nose is broken, and I expect his pride as well, but they'll mend, they'll mend." He chuckled.

"I did not mean Lord Westbridge, I meant Mr. Buckley," Elizabeth said reproachfully.

The doctor lost his smile and his demeanor became grave. "Ah, Mr. Buckley. I am afraid it is too soon to tell; he has not yet regained consciousness. You see, he has suffered a nasty knock on the temple, and there is probably a concussion. Outside of that, he has suffered no other injury, which is quite remarkable considering what his lordship looks like. Of course, I did have to tape his knuckles, which were rather scratched up, but I thought certain Mr. Buckley's nose was broken, too, when I saw the blood streaming out of it earlier, and it was not even dented. What a fight! It is as though his lordship never laid a hand upon him. Won quite a pretty bit of money on that one, I did, but then I've always prided myself on being able to pick a winner. I have often said—"

"May I see him?" Elizabeth interrupted impatiently.

"His lordship requested no visitors."

"Mr. Buckley!" Elizabeth exclaimed.

"Oh, of course, of course," the doctor said hastily. "In fact, I think it would be a good idea if someone remained with him at all times until he awakens. There is no telling in a case like this."

"I will be happy to do that, doctor," Mrs. Locke said readily.

136

"No, Auntie, I'd rather it was I," Elizabeth said.

"My dear girl, you need some sleep—you look as though you haven't closed your eyes for a fortnight," her aunt said.

"I shan't sleep anyway, not until I know that Charlie is better," Elizabeth insisted. "At least let me sit with him now, while you are at dinner. I couldn't eat anything anyway."

"Very well," Mrs. Locke agreed reluctantly, and the doctor led them into Charlie's room.

He was asleep, or unconscious, on the bed, his head wrapped in a white bandage. Elizabeth felt her heart rise in her throat when she saw how pale and vulnerable he looked, and she had to suppress an impossible desire to gather him in her arms and kiss the injury away.

"There is no external wound, you understand," the doctor was explaining in a low voice, "but a bandage wrapped tightly around the head contains the pressure caused by such an injury. I expect he will have a nasty bruise, if he comes to."

Elizabeth did not care for his use of the word "if." She went over to the window, where there was a cozy window seat, and turned to the doctor. "Is it all right if I open the draperies?" she asked him.

"Now that it is dark, there would be no harm in it, but do be sure to close them in the morning, for a bright light would be most injurious. And whatever you do, do not open the window. The night air is poison, especially to one in his condition."

Elizabeth reflected whimsically that the doctor and Lord Westbridge must have dealt together famously, for their notions of what was healthful or unhealthful seemed to coincide. She pushed back the draperies, and upon hearing her aunt gasp turned around in alarm, certain that Charlie had gone into convulsions at the very least.

"Doctor, you may leave us now," her aunt said quickly. "There is something I wish to say to my niece."

"Of course, of course," he said amiably—something seemed to have pleased him recently. "Now, do be sure and call me the minute he awakens."

When he was gone Elizabeth looked at her aunt questioningly.

"Elizabeth!" Mrs. Locke hissed in a loud whisper. "Where is your petticoat? I can see your—your *limbs* quite clearly silhouetted in the window, and I am sure the doctor saw them, too."

"Ah, that explains his expression." Elizabeth smiled.

"You have not answered my question! Where is your petticoat? If you tell me Lord Westbridge removed it, I will have a stroke right here before your eyes!"

"I lost it," Elizabeth said, unconcerned.

"Lost it! How does one *lose* a petticoat?" her aunt demanded.

Elizabeth almost laughed, but remembered in time that it might disturb Charlie. "Why, I took it off when Charlie fell, to rest his head upon," she explained reasonably.

Her aunt was not satisfied. "I thought he fell directly the fight was over."

"So he did, and I rushed into the middle of the ring and put my petticoat under his head. But don't ask me where it has got to since then, for as I said I have lost it."

"You took your petticoat off in the middle of the boxing ring?" Mrs. Locke had turned quite pink from the effort of not speaking above a whisper.

"I suppose I did," Elizabeth replied mildly.

"In front of the whole town?"

"Do you think the whole town was there?" Elizabeth asked with an expression of interest. "I had no idea boxing was such a popular sport."

"That is not the point! The point is, you disrobed in public! It is one thing to run off with a nobleman when you are betrothed to another and have your entire family follow you, posthaste! That can be attributed to nothing more than youthful high spirits. But to disrobe

138

in public! That shows a complete want of delicacy and decency that are expected in one who has been gently brought up, as you have been. Elizabeth, I despair of you!" She put her hands to her head in agitation.

"I am sorry, Auntie," Elizabeth said.

"And well you might be!" Mrs. Locke declared. "I am going downstairs now to eat my dinner, if I can possibly manage more than one bite after what you have told me. Charles appears to be perfectly comfortable, so I trust you will not find it necessary to remove any more of your garments to add to his comfort."

"Certainly not, Auntie," Elizabeth promised, and Mrs. Locke left, shaking her head all the while.

Elizabeth turned back to look out the window momentarily, but the view to be had was not very interesting, and try as she might she could not keep her gaze from wandering back to Charlie, lying so quietly in his bed. Finally, she gave in to her urges and knelt beside him, stroking his hair tenderly and smoothing it down so that it almost hid the bandage.

He looked so young, like a sleeping boy who had not a care in the world. And yet, even in repose, there was a certain strength in his face, especially in the line of his jaw. She ran her fingers gently along his cheek, feeling the faint, invisible stubble of his fair beard.

"Charlie," she whispered. "Charlie, can you ever forgive me? I have been such a fool." She buried her face against his shoulder as she felt the tears well up in her eyes. "Charlie, please get better," she whispered. "If only you will get better I will never bother you again. I will never argue with you, or be cross, or call you names—never, ever again. I shall go away and you need never see me again, and then you can find some other girl who is worthy of you."

She lifted her head again, but Charlie slept on, so she reached up and kissed him gently on the lips. "I don't blame you for never wanting to do that when you were awake," she whispered. "What a selfish beast I have been. And I will never blame you if you never,

139

ever want to do it in the future. I shall go off some place where you will not ever have to see me again and you can live your life in peace. I doubt that I shall ever marry now, for I doubt that I could ever love anyone as much as I love you."

Charlie slept on.

"Charlie, please get well!" And she buried her face in the bedclothes so no one could hear the sound of her sobs.

# ELEVEN

Richard Tanner entered the breakfast room the next morning remarkably light of heart for one whose closest friend lay in a coma in a room just above his head. However, Richard was not unduly worried about Charles; while the report he had just received from Jemmy Breadlow indicated that there was no change in the patient, Richard had faith in his friend's strong constitution and was confident it would take more than a knock on the head to do him in.

So he hummed as he entered the private dining room, until he discovered it was occupied only by Mr. Locke, reading a newspaper.

"Morning, Tanner," he said, politely folding the paper and putting it aside.

"Pray, do not stop on my account," Mr. Tanner told him as he helped himself to a plateful of eggs and kippers. "It has always been my policy not to make intelligent conversation before noon."

"Nothing in it, anyway," Mr. Locke said, disgusted. "Nothing but Whigs and Tories, Tories and Whigs, the king's health failing and worries about the succession. Same old thing."

"Indeed," Mr. Tanner said as he sat down and attacked his breakfast with a hearty appetite. "Hardly worth wasting the paper and ink to print it, eh?"

"Exactly," Mr. Locke said, flicking the offending

publication with his finger. "That young chap, Jemmy something-or-other, tells me you might be going on to London today."

"My original plan had been to stop here only one night," Mr. Tanner admitted, "but that was before I discovered one of the few people I wished to visit in London was stopping here as well. I believe it is no more than my duty as a friend to remain here until Charles has recovered his health."

"Quite so," Mr. Locke agreed. "But it is too bad, nonetheless. I am returning to London myself this morning and would have liked the company. Nothing to keep me here, you know. The wife has it all under control and I must see to my affairs in town."

"Of course," Mr. Tanner said between bites.

Mr. Locke gave the newspaper one last disparaging glance, finished off his tea, and arose. "Well, I'm off, then. Very pleasant meeting you, Tanner. Hope we will meet again in town."

Richard murmured, "Of course," again, and Mr. Locke left him alone, still muttering, "Whigs and Tories, Tories and Whigs. They'll all anarchists if you ask me."

Richard rang the bell for a fresh pot of tea, and when Molly answered his summons he asked her in a studiously nonchalant manner, "Have any of the young ladies come down yet?"

"Miss Durant is sitting with the poor young gentleman again," Molly told him readily, "and Mrs. Locke is helping me mum in the kitchen, preparing some kind of broth for him when he awakes." She wrinkled her nose. "And doesn't it smell half bad, too? Poor soul, I hope they don't try to ladle too much down him at once. Here, Mr. Tanner, I'll just warm that up for you." She took the teapot and was about to leave.

"And what of the other young ladies, Molly? Are they taking breakfast in their rooms or do you expect them to come down?"

"I took a tray up to the blancmangey one, Miss Locke, as she's called, not this half hour past. But the other—I'm afraid I can't pronounce her name—I expect she'll be down, because she called for her maid nearly an hour ago. And not a moment too soon, I can tell you, Mr. Tanner, for that Spanish hussy has been making eyes at my Jemmy ever since she got here, and if Mr. Locke's man weren't leaving with Mr. Locke for London we'd see another bout of fisticuffs in this town, I can tell you. I shan't be a minute with this tea, Mr. Tanner."

He rose and helped himself to another plate of eggs, hoping to make his breakfast last until Miss DelSorro's expected entrance.

She arrived shortly after Molly had returned with a fresh pot of tea, and the delighted expression on Richard Tanner's face gave some clue as to why he had been humming earlier. Francesca, too, seemed quite pleased about something that morning, and while Richard would have liked to think himself the cause of her radiant smile, he did not doubt there was some other reason behind her good humor.

"A very fine day, is it not, Mr. Tanner?" Francesca said as she took a seat opposite him and poured herself some tea.

He was very fond of the way she had of rolling her r's. "Indeed it is, Miss DelSorro," he agreed. "Perhaps, if you have nothing better to do, you might care to walk through the town with me. A very fine view can be had from the top of the knoll overlooking the village, and the church is a fine example of Norman architecture."

"That would be lovely, Mr. Tanner," she said. "I have no plans other than ministering to the wounded, and *that* should not take very long, as his injuries have made him quite cross."

"Charlie is awake then?" Richard asked her eagerly.

"Oh, no, unfortunately not. I was speaking of Lord Westbridge."

"Of course," he said, disappointed.

"Charlie is well looked after by Elizabeth, who slept like a bottom last night," Francesca told him.

"I beg your pardon?"

"Does not one say 'I slept like a top' when one has

143

had a very good night's rest?" she inquired, and Richard nodded. "Well, then, Elizabeth did not sleep at all well, so she must have slept like a bottom."

He could not dispute her logic.

"I shared a bed with her, you see, and that is how I know she slept like a bottom. Which is exactly how it should be," she added with satisfaction.

"Naturally, she was worried about Charlie," Richard said.

"Naturally," Francesca agreed. "Bah—this tea! As much as I drink it, I cannot grow accustomed to it. Have you finished your breakfast, Mr. Tanner? I think I am ready for that walk you promised me."

"But you have eaten nothing yet, Miss DelSorro. I would certainly be happy to wait for you until you have."

"I rarely eat breakfast, Mr. Tanner. It produces most unpleasant effects in my digestive system. I have only to fetch my hat and gloves and I will be quite ready to accompany you."

"You are not going to look in on Lord Westbridge then?" he asked hopefully.

"I have already done so, which is how I can attest to his ill temper," she said with a smile. "I will wait until this afternoon before I brave the lion's den again."

They met a few minutes later in front of the inn, and Francesca took Richard's arm as they strolled off.

"You are a great friend of Charlie's, are you not?" she asked him presently.

"I was his tutor during his last year at Oxford, and we became friends then."

"He is very clever, is he not?" Francesca asked.

"Oh, certainly," Richard said.

"Then you must be more clever yet, Mr. Tanner, to have taught him."

He laughed slightly. "I know more *facts*, as I am a few years older than he, but I can tell you, Miss DelSorro, if he had remained at Oxford much longer he would soon have been teaching me."

"I do hope his mind is not affected by his injury,"

144

Francesca said. "It would be too bad, especially after all my other plans have gone so well."

"I beg your pardon?" Mr. Tanner asked. He wondered if it was because of a faulty knowledge of the English language that Miss DelSorro had so much trouble making herself understood to him.

She smiled up at him, a brilliant smile that won his heart all over again. "Mr. Tanner, I like you. I liked you as soon as I met you last night, and because I like you, and because you are a great friend of Charlie's and because you are also a disinterested party, I am going to confide in you. I will burst otherwise; it is always so difficult to keep one's successes to oneself. I have never been very good at it."

"Miss DelSorro, I would feel honored if you were to make me the recipient of your confidences," he said gallantly, though he was mystified as to what those confidences might be and did not choose to point out, either, that he did not plan to remain a disinterested party long.

"Mr. Tanner, it is all my doing that we are here today," she said importantly.

Richard remained polite, although he had a sudden, awful suspicion that perhaps Miss DelSorro was not quite sane and harbored delusions of divinity; but he was determined to hear her out to the end. The stirrings he had felt in his breast upon his first sight of the lady were of a nature that could not be ignored, and perhaps if she was insane his steadfast love could return her to herself.

"Perhaps it will be easier to explain if I begin at the beginning," she said. "You see, when I arrived in this country, I soon learned that Elizabeth thought she was in love with Ivor. If he had offered for her right away, as he should have done, she would soon have learned her error. But instead Ivor did not behave quite as he should have, so Elizabeth engaged herself to Charles, whom she is really in love with but did not know it. Of course, I guessed it the first time I saw them together, and at least Charles knew he was in love with *her* right

145

from the start, which made my task a good deal easier. But it is too bad they became engaged when they did."

Richard was glad to hear her speak in such a rational tone of voice, although what she spoke about still bore the traces of deep-seated lunacy. "If Elizabeth is really in love with Charles, as you say, what then was wrong with their engagement?" he asked.

"Because she still thought she was in love with Ivor!" Francesca exclaimed. "By engaging herself to Charles, she thought she was taking second-best, and so would she think for all the rest of her life unless something occurred to make her realize that she did not love Ivor after all."

Richard wondered if insanity was catching, for what Francesca was saying was actually beginning to make sense to him.

"That is when I put my finger in the cake," Francesca continued. "First, I showed Ivor where he had gone wrong and how he must treat Elizabeth with special attention so that she would break her engagement to Charles and engage herself to Ivor." She gave a slight sigh. "But I am afraid that didn't work very well, for Ivor has very little notion of what will please a lady of Elizabeth's disposition. He did not send her a single nosegay, as I expressly told him to do. I don't mind too much about the books of poetry he did not send, but a single nosegay was not too much to ask, was it?"

"Of course not," Richard agreed, certain by now that he had gone completely mad and it didn't really matter what he said.

"I saw that drastic action was needed, for Elizabeth could not make up her mind one way or the other. So I visited Ivor on Monday afternoon and convinced him that the only thing for him to do was to steal Elizabeth away and marry her immediately. Then I told Charles that Ivor had abducted her so that he would follow them, and they would fight and Elizabeth would realize she really loved Charles, and all would be well. And for the most part, everything has gone quite according to plan."

146

"You have missed your calling, Miss DelSorro," Richard said with admiration, pleased to find the clear light of sanity returning to him. "You should have been a great tactician, a leader of men, a general."

"Are you implying that I am not?" Francesca asked him with a pointed look.

"Certainly not!" he declared. "But tell me, how were you so certain the two men would fight?"

"You are not acquainted with Lord Westbridge, as I am," Francesca told him. "In matters of honor, he is always—the stick?"

"A stickler?" he supplied.

"Yes, quite so. Elizabeth taught me that word," she mentioned as an aside. "Of course, I had thought it would be pistols or swords, in which case Charles would have certainly lost, as he was meant to."

"Miss DelSorro, please do not think I am challenging your knowledge of human nature," Richard put in. "But since it was your desire for Elizabeth to end up with Charles, wouldn't it have been better if he were to win the fight, as indeed he did?"

"Oh, no!" Francesca exclaimed. "You see, Elizabeth is English." She stopped as if that were all the explanation needed.

"That cannot be denied," Richard admitted, "but what is that to the point?"

"Why, she has the typical English character, which is to support the lower hound."

"Underdog?" he prompted.

"Underdog! You see, Mr. Tanner, as the victor, Ivor would appear to Elizabeth as a bully and a brute, while Charles, the loser, would need comforting and consolation. But to give credit where it is due, Charles has improved upon my plan. First he won, which might have turned Elizabeth against him, but then he tripped and hurt himself most seriously. So now Elizabeth has the double satisfaction of siding with the victor while at the same time comforting him as though he had been the loser. Of course, it will all be for nothing if he has lost his mind because of it," she concluded gloomily.

"Let me see if I understand you correctly," Richard said. "Are you implying that Charles fell and hurt his head deliberately?"

"No, not at all!" Francesca assured him. "But it could not have been managed better if he had."

"This is most enlightening," Richard said with a smile. "I see I have been shut up with my books for too long when my time might have been put to more profit as a student of human nature, as you appear to be."

"And now it must be clear to you why I was so pleased that Elizabeth passed a restless night," Francesca said. "It can mean nothing else but that she has finally realized she is in love with Charles. When he awakens, her love will be shining out of her eyes like a beacon, and they will make it up and propose to live happily evermore."

"Admirable!" Richard said with feeling. "A most happy ending to an exciting love affair."

They had reached the crest of the hill and now paused to admire the view.

"I find this little village most charming," Francesca remarked presently. "If one must have an accident on the road, one could not choose a more delightful spot. Nonetheless, I am disappointed that Elizabeth and Ivor did not reach Westham Park."

"Surely that makes little difference in the outcome of your plan," Richard said.

"I suppose not," she agreed and shrugged, "but I should have liked to have seen it, to see what changes I might care to make one day in the furnishings or grounds."

Having just satisfied himself that Miss DelSorro was sound of mind, Richard was disturbed by this new evidence of mental infirmity.

She noticed his confusion and laughed. "But of course, I have not told you the rest of my plan, Mr. Tanner. Did you think I would make no provision for myself? I am to marry Lord Westbridge. Indeed, it is what I came to England to do—I have loved him since I was a child."

Richard was not precisely pleased by this information.

"That is why it was so important to show Elizabeth she did not love Ivor," Francesca explained, "else she might have been jealous and resentful of me to the ends of our days. Now, I hope, all will proceed smoothly. Is that the church you mentioned?" she asked, pointing. "It looks most interesting; let us visit it."

Richard followed her back down the hill, a slight frown creasing his brow.

"Miss DelSorro, might I ask how, after expending all your energies to convince Lord Westbridge that he was in love with your cousin, you plan to convince him he is in love with you?"

"That will be easy," she said, throwing him a sparkling smile which gave him good reason to believe her. "I have already begun the process by nursing him most tenderly, and while the rest of my plan is not yet firm, I have an idea that I would like to sing for him."

"Sing for him? You are a singer, then, as well as a—strategist," he stopped himself just in time from saying "meddler."

"Yes," she said, then a few moments later she stopped and turned to him suddenly. "Mr. Tanner! I have just remembered where I have heard your name before. Are you not the friend of Charlie's who knows a great deal about opera?"

"I have made something of a study of it," he admitted.

"Do you think you could advise me on choosing a program? And of course, I will need a great deal of practice, as I am sadly out of voice."

Richard regarded her quizzically. He disliked the idea of helping her to win another man's heart and did not even know if her voice was worth the trouble, but the great deal of practice she needed might give him an opportunity to spend a great deal of time in her company, time he might find profitable in advancing some plans of his own.

"I should be delighted to be of service in any way I can, Miss DelSorro," he said.

"You are more than kind!" she declared happily.

149

"Soon Ivor will realize he needn't look very far for his duchess."

Richard was glad that was the last time he heard her mention that name this morning, for he was feeling most disturbing sensations of jealousy. But before he allowed these sensations to manifest themselves, he turned the conversation to opera, where he found Francesca most knowledgeable, and as they explored the church they also spoke of architecture, where she was less knowledgeable but eager to learn. They were soon joined by Mr. Hopewell, the rector, who had spied them out of the rectory window and delighted in relating the history of his parish to strangers. They were asked to return later to take tea with him and Mrs. Hopewell and accepted most graciously, and all the time Richard Tanner was wondering if Miss DelSorro's machinations *always* turned out as she planned.

Charles Buckley awoke to a loud ringing in his ears. At first he thought it was church bells, and that he was being privileged to witness his own funeral, but the throbbing pain in his head gave the lie to the supposition that he was dead. Gradually, he realized that the ringing was inside his head as well, a direct result of the throbbing, and soon it dawned on him that the dim blur which was all he could see was not part of a cloud he was passing through on his voyage to the heavenly gates, but merely a ceiling, rendered featureless because he was not wearing his spectacles.

With an effort he turned his head toward the only source of light in the room, and stared for some time until the shape that was silhouetted there resolved itself into his cousin's form.

"Lizzie?" he called out weakly, and was surprised at the amount of effort it took to do so.

Elizabeth immediately put down the book she was reading and came to his side.

"Charlie! Thank God you are awake at last. We have been so worried. How are you feeling? No, do not speak. Keep still and I will go for the doctor."

150

She turned toward the door, but Charlie made a feeble gesture to stay her.

"Wait, don't go," he said. "Please—tell me what has happened." He put his hand to his head as if the effort to remember made it ache all the more. "I thought I had finished Westbridge off completely. Did he take a foul shot at me or what?"

"Certainly not," Elizabeth told him. "You tripped on his foot."

"Tripped on his foot?" he repeated, disbelieving. He pondered this for a moment.

"Westbridge was much too busy writhing in pain to take a foul shot," Elizabeth said. "In fact, he could hardly lift his head. I believe you broke his nose." She could not hide the note of pride that crept into her voice.

"And I tripped on his foot?" Charlie asked again, pressing his fingers to his head to discover the extent of his injury and wincing when he found the sore spot. "Must have given you all a good laugh, eh?"

Elizabeth frowned. "*I* did not laugh. I saw nothing to laugh about in the whole exhibition, from start to finish."

"Come closer, Lizzie, I cannot hear you without my spectacles," Charlie said somewhat illogically. "Where are they?"

Elizabeth picked them up from the side table, but hesitated before she gave them to him. "I am not certain you should have these. The doctor does not want you to strain your eyes in any way, as it would not be good for your head."

"Nonsense!" he said, a little louder than he should have for his own comfort. He made an effort to sit up, but fell back dizzily.

"You must not try to move," Elizabeth warned him belatedly, adjusting his pillows for him.

"I strain my eyes a good deal more by not being able to see clearly," Charlie pointed out, enjoying her ministrations.

151

"Very well, here you are," she said. "I do hope you are not going to be a difficult patient."

He felt a little better once he was able to put the room into clear focus and take stock of his surroundings.

"It is lucky you were not wearing those when you fell or they might have smashed and put your eye out," Elizabeth said.

"If I had been wearing them, I would have seen his blasted foot," Charlie said ruefully. "What time is it, Lizzie? What *day* is it?"

"It is about two o'clock in the afternoon," she told him. "You have been unconscious for about eighteen hours."

"Ah, that explains why I feel so hungry."

"If you will let me go and send for the doctor, I will bring you something to eat, too."

He made a weak attempt at a smile. "No invalid food, though—I could do with something substantial."

"I will see what the doctor says," Elizabeth replied. She paused at the doorway. "If it will make you feel any better, Ivor has been in bed all day, too, after the trouncing you gave him. Now, do not move a muscle until the doctor gets here."

# TWELVE

Elizabeth returned shortly with a tray containing some broth and bread. "The doctor has been sent for, but evidently he is attending a birth at a nearby farm, so he may be some time," she said. "In the meanwhile, I have brought you your luncheon—or breakfast—or whatever you may choose to call it."

"It looks suspiciously like invalid food to me," Charlie said, eyeing the tray with misgiving.

"Do not complain," Elizabeth said tartly. "Aunt Annabel has been all day in the kitchen preparing it for you." She set the tray down on the side table and readjusted his pillows so he could sit up to eat. "Do you want me to feed you or do you think you can manage on your own?" she asked.

"I think I can manage if you will hold the edge of the tray so it won't wobble."

Elizabeth sat on the bed next to him and balanced the tray on his lap, keeping a hold on it as requested.

"Why is Aunt Annabel here?" Charlie asked presently, after sampling the broth and finding it quite tasty. "It sounds as if this elopement of yours has turned into quite a family outing."

"I do not think you should talk so much," Elizabeth said shortly.

"Then I won't, if you will just answer my question and tell me all that has happened since last night."

153

She outlined briefly for him the events that had occurred since his fall the night before; but while Charlie was interested in her tale, he might have been even more interested in what she left out than in what she related to him in a flat, expressionless voice.

For she made no mention of that ghastly moment when she had thought him dead, nor how she had discovered it is quite true that one's life seems to flash before one's eyes in moments of crisis. Neither did she describe how she had removed her petticoat in front of the whole town and her aunt's subsequent horror upon discovering the fact, although that part of the story would have amused him.

She knew, though, that he would certainly not be amused by the story of her own sleepless night. After attending his two other patients again after dinner, the doctor had given Elizabeth a few drops of laudanum to help her sleep, but they proved ineffective. She was too overcome by a terrible feeling of guilt, the knowledge that if Charlie never awoke it would be entirely due to her childish behavior. "If only" became the theme of her mental self-abuse. If only she had not run off with Westbridge, Charlie would not have followed to fight with him. If only she had not agreed to marry Charlie, she would not have had to run off with Westbridge. If only she had not tried to trick Westbridge, Charlie would not have proposed to her in the first place. If only Emma had not goaded her so, she would not have felt the need to rush Westbridge.

The slight comfort that all her troubles could be laid at Emma's door soothed her long enough to gain about two hours of sleep, but the dream that came to her was almost worse than lying awake.

She dreamed she was walking down the aisle of a church with Ivor, still wearing her bedraggled ball gown, grimy and sweaty and petticoatless. Her feet moved with reluctance, as though she were treading through treacle. When they reached the altar, she noticed that the priest was Charles himself, his head

154

wrapped in a plaster and his eyes staring and glazed. He held the prayer book in his hands and intoned as if reading from it, but his words made no sense.

"It is all because you broke my parasol, you know," Elizabeth told him in the dream. "You were always breaking my things." Her voice was that of the twelve-year-old Elizabeth, bossy and the least bit shrill.

"Keep quiet or you will have no bathwater for a week," Ivor told her harshly.

"Nonsense, I always get what I want," Elizabeth retorted. "Father sees to that." But when she looked around her father was not there, and she was frightened.

"He won't help you," Ivor growled. "He knows what you have done to Charles and he hates you for it."

"No! I didn't do it. It was Emma! Emma did it!" the now six-year-old Elizabeth cried out. "She's always doing things! I wouldn't hurt Charlie, it was Emma pushed him off the gate. I wouldn't hurt Charlie—I love him! It was Emma!"

But when Elizabeth awoke in a cold sweat she knew that she could not blame her cousin for what had happened today. She had only her own selfishness and blindness to blame. And blind indeed she had been. Why had it been necessary for Charlie to risk his life before she realized he was worth more to her than a dozen Westbridges? Why had she not seen it after the weeks of almost daily exposure to his kindness and good sense and quietly noble nature? She should have recognized that noble nature the night he proposed to her, for she could see now that he had done it only to help her save face after her rejection by Westbridge.

Too late had she learned that all her fanciful, romantic ideals of what she wanted in a husband were actually based on her childhood love for Charles, which had finally grown to maturity. Too late did she pause to consider what life would be like without him, for Charlie was always there, had always been there. But now she would have to learn to live without him, for she could not allow him to sacrifice himself on the altar of her selfishness. She could not allow him to marry her out of pity.

But she revealed none of this to Charles in her narrative, for it was too late, too late. He would be perfectly justified in never speaking to her again, instead of listening to her attentively and trying to be cheerful so that she would not know he was in pain and feeling quite wretched.

"And I understand your friend Mr. Tanner and Francesca took a long walk together this morning and were invited back to the rectory for tea," she finished. "They seem to be getting on quite well together."

"I am glad," Charlie said. He put his spoon down and laid back with a sigh.

Elizabeth took up the tray and said with false brightness, "What happened to that ravenous appetite you boasted of before? You have finished only half your soup."

"I suppose I was not as hungry as I thought," he said, and closed his eyes.

"I am going to see what is keeping that doctor," she said. "Surely he could have delivered quadruplets in all this time."

"Thank you, Lizzie," he said with a brief smile.

"I will look in on you again after dinner. Perhaps I can read to you then, if you like."

"Yes, I would like that."

Elizabeth went off with a worried frown, which eased only slightly when she met the doctor coming up the stairs. She deposited the tray in the kitchen and told her aunt of her intention to take a nap until dinnertime, so that she could sit with Charles during the night if necessary.

Elizabeth was awakened from her nap several hours later when Francesca came in with her maid to dress for dinner. Francesca apologized for disturbing her, but was eager to tell her of the lovely day she had spent with Mr. Tanner.

156

"He is quite a gentleman, considering that he is a teacher at university," Francesca chattered to her cousin, "and he is quite clever and knows all manner of things. But Elizabeth, is it not wonderful what the doctor has said about Charlie?"

"What did he say?" Elizabeth asked eagerly. "I am afraid I was too tired to wait until he had finished his examination."

"He says there is no permanent damage and all Charlie needs a few days' rest and he will be right as a—triplet?"

"Trivet," Elizabeth said with a little laugh. "That is indeed wonderful news."

"It certainly is!" Francesca agreed. "As for Ivor, his injuries are more obvious, but he is quite well enough to join us for dinner tonight."

Elizabeth did not greet this news with quite as much enthusiasm, for she was nervous about meeting Lord Westbridge again. He, too, had a perfect right never to speak to her again, and while such a prospect did not exactly fill her with dismay, it might make the conversation at dinner rather awkward.

She left Francesca to the ministrations of Conchita and wandered down to the common room, finding she was the first one there except for two local farmers seated in the corner, in the midst of a heated discussion about pigs. Elizabeth acknowledged them with a brief nod. Someone had left a book open on one of the side tables, and she picked it up idly and leafed through it. The inscription inside the cover indicated that it belonged to Richard Tanner, and she opened it to read a few passages, to discover if it was something that might interest Charlie. But the sound of a coach pulling up before the inn interrupted her and brought her to the window, as she wondered if yet another guest could be accommodated, the place was so full with the followers of her elopement.

To her surprise the coach contained Nigel Foxmoor, and after giving his instructions to the coachman, he came inside.

"Mr. Foxmoor," Elizabeth greeted him. "This is a pleasant surprise. What brings you to this tiny village?"

"Miss Durant," he said, bowing to her briefly. "I am very glad indeed I found you. I ran into your uncle at the club and he told me where you all could be found. Dashed funny sort of place for a holiday, I should have said." He looked around and obviously did not think too much of the furnishings.

"I expect you want to see Miss DelSorro," Elizabeth said. "She is still dressing for dinner and will be down soon. You timed your arrival quite well, for we are to dine soon. If you like, I will go and tell her you are here."

"No, no, don't wish to be any trouble," he said quickly. "Who do I see about getting a room?"

"Mr. Currier is the owner; you might find him in the taproom. I believe the others are all busy preparing our meal. Perhaps you would care to sit down. I see they have put something out for us—I expect it is sherry." She walked over to the table, where a decanter and a number of glasses had been placed.

"No need to trouble yourself, Miss Durant. I'll do the honors. Would you care for a glass yourself?" He sniffed the contents of the decanter. "It is sherry, most assuredly. Dry, I should say."

"Thank you, I could do with a glass," Elizabeth admitted. "But are you quite sure you wouldn't like me to tell Miss DelSorro you are here? I know she always takes such a time dressing."

He poured her a glass and handed it to her, hemming and hawing that it really wasn't necessary and trying to explain why not, until he was interrupted by Francesca herself.

"My dear Elizabeth, it is not I he has come to see," she said, laughing in the doorway. "Is that not right, Cousin Nigel?"

"Nonsense," Nigel declared stoutly. "It is always a pleasure to see you, Miss DelSorro. Some sherry?"

"Thank you," Francesca said. "Do sit down, Elizabeth; it makes me nervous when you pace so." She turned back to Nigel with a brilliant smile. "Miss Locke should be down shortly, but I doubt you will have time to speak to her before dinner."

"That is quite all right," Nigel said cheerfully. "It can wait, it can wait."

Elizabeth looked at them both with confusion, first at Francesca, then at Nigel.

"Do you mean . . . ?" she began.

Francesca interrupted, "Tell me, Cousin Nigel, how were you clever enough to find us?"

"I was just telling Miss Durant, I ran into Mr. Locke at the club at luncheon." He creased his brow. "Knew there was something I'd forgotten! He told me Buckley had had an accident. I do hope he is all right?"

"The doctor says he will be quite well in a week or so," Francesca told him.

"Then that is all right," Nigel said with relief. "Dashed rum thing to happen on your holiday, I must say. I suppose I can look in on him later on?"

"I rather think he will be glad of the company," Elizabeth said.

"Did Mr. Locke tell you that Lord Westbridge was also involved in this *accident*?" Francesca asked cautiously.

"No!" Nigel exclaimed. "Westbridge, too? There isn't a curse on this place, is there? I shouldn't have come if there is—shouldn't like anything to happen to my horses."

"Oh, the accident did not involve horses," Francesca said and laughed, "so you need have no fears on that score. But perhaps it would be best if you did not question Lord Westbridge about it when he comes down, for it was a most painful experience for him, as you can imagine." She glanced toward Elizabeth, who was studying one of the hunting prints on the wall.

"Certainly, certainly, you can depend on me, Miss DelSorro."

"And here is Lord Westbridge now!" Francesca said,

rising to greet him. "How pleasant to see you out of bed, my lord, and looking so well."

This was a gross exaggeration, for Lord Westbridge looked anything but well. He had a piece of plaster across his nose, and both his eyes were discolored and swollen, and the obstreperous expression on his face did nothing to soften the rather alarming appearance he made.

"Miss DelSorro. Mr. Foxmoor. Miss Durant," he greeted them all in turn.

Elizabeth mumbled something nervously in reply, and when she finally forced herself to look him square in the face, she had to stifle a sudden and disturbing urge to laugh.

Mrs. Locke bustled in, putting an end to the awkward moment. "My dear Francesca," she said, in a dither, "you really must keep a closer eye on that maidservant of yours. She has been in the coachhouse entertaining the grooms in a most improper manner, I am told."

Francesca laughed. "I will see to it," she said. "I always told Papa that Conchita would not do well in England. She has always been too high-spirited."

"Is that what they call it in Spain?" Mrs. Locke said with a sniff as Francesca left to make peace in the servants' quarters. "Why, Mr. Foxmoor, what a pleasant surprise to see you here."

"Mrs. Locke," he said, bowing graciously over her hand. "Your husband told me today that you had all come on holiday here, and although it seems a dashed strange place to have a holiday, I hope you don't mind my joining you."

"Of course not," she replied. "In fact, we are rather short of men and your presence will make our numbers more even. You are dining with us, are you not? Good. I will go tell Molly to lay another place." She passed her daughter on her way out of the door. "Emma, my dear, it is about time you joined us. Look who is here."

Emma had appeared to be rather grumpy until she

160

saw Nigel; then an almost magical transformation took place. Her eyes brightened, the downturned ends of her mouth turned up in a most delightful smile, and her complexion took on a rosy hue that was well set off by the pink frock she was wearing. Elizabeth watched with fascination as the two were drawn to each other, exchanging few words, each content merely to gaze into the other's eyes.

Francesca returned shortly with Mr. Tanner, who had met her in the hallway and helpfully supplied Conchita with several of his shirts to mend, although, as Francesca pointed out, she was very rapid with her needle and could not be depended upon to stay out of trouble for long. Mrs. Locke then returned to say that dinner was ready, and as the company were all assembled, they might as well go in immediately.

"I have become an impresario," Mr. Tanner told them all presently as they were eating the simple but hearty fare Mrs. Currier had provided.

His announcement was greeted with the requisite murmurs of curiosity.

"Miss DelSorro had been kind enough to allow me to arrange a little concert for her," he explained. "She wishes to invite only the closest friends, of course, so I think it will be a simple matter to produce. That is, if the idea meets with your approval, madam."

"Certainly," Mrs. Locke said, pleased by his deference. "I had no idea you were a singer, Francesca. You should have told us and we would have been certain to have heard you before now."

"I am sadly out of practice, cousin," Francesca said, "and I do not care to sing before company unless they are expressly gathered for the purpose of hearing me." Emma did not see the pointed glance that was directed toward her, for she was too wrapped up in Mr. Foxmoor. "However," Francesca continued, "I think several weeks' practice will put me in voice again, and Mr. Tanner has been kind enough to promise to arrange it all. He knows of an excellent teacher of voice in London."

"Why, that is wonderful," Mrs. Locke said enthusiastically. "I had planned to hold at least one more reception before the end of the season, and I think this will prove to be just the thing. I must make a list of those we should invite."

"Everyone who is here present, of course," Francesca said, smiling significantly across the table at Westbridge.

"It is unfortunate that Charles has been injured," Mr. Tanner said, "for he would have made a fine accompanist. However, I know of someone else who would be most willing to oblige."

"Yes, of course," Elizabeth said. "I had almost forgotten how Charlie always used to play for us at our country parties. I have not heard him play for a long time."

"He, too, is one who dislikes public performance," Mr. Tanner said. "At least of his piano playing," he added with a quick glance at Westbridge, who squirmed uncomfortably. "Of course, like Miss DelSorro, he sets high standards for himself, and will only perform when he is certain he will do well."

Elizabeth hid a smile behind her napkin, and Francesca, too, had to acknowledge that Mr. Tanner had most successfully hit his target, even though her sympathies necessarily lay with Westbridge at the moment. Noticing that his lordship was not about to take this remark gracefully, Francesca inclined her head toward him and inquired if he had any preference for what she might sing.

"I have never professed any knowledge of music whatsoever," Ivor said shortly.

"I have been thinking about just that all afternoon," Mr. Tanner interrupted smoothly, "and I have come up with a few suggestions. Perhaps we could discuss it further after dinner, Miss DelSorro."

"It would be a pleasure, Mr. Tanner," she replied. "If one chooses a good program, even those with no tutored tastes for music will find they enjoy it quite as well." She smiled reassuringly at Ivor.

After dinner Elizabeth took up the book that was still lying in the common room and asked Mr. Tanner, "I promised Charlie I would read to him. Do you think this book would interest him?"

"Certainly not!" he said with a laugh. "That is a book of exceedingly dull sermons written by a friend of mine and which I am reading only for friendship's sake. I have a copy of *Guy Mannering* upstairs which I think both of you will find much more interesting. I will go and fetch it."

"Thank you," Elizabeth said gratefully.

He returned in a matter of minutes with three slim volumes, and Elizabeth was about to go upstairs and see if Charles indeed wished to be read to when Lord Westbridge approached her.

"Miss Durant," he said abruptly, "I wish to speak to you. I am planning to leave this place as early as possible tomorrow morning, and I think we should discuss a few things before I return to London. Would you walk outside with me for a moment?"

Elizabeth looked around helplessly, as if another member of the company would come to her rescue, but no one was paying the least attention to their exchange. Reluctantly, for she was dreading this interview, she agreed.

"Miss Durant," he said when they had walked but a few paces, "I cannot ever hope for you to forgive my precipitate behavior in abducting you."

She had expected an upbraiding, not an apology, and was pleasantly surprised.

"It was not exactly an abduction, my lord," she pointed out. "I did come with you willingly."

"Yes, quite so. And my intentions were entirely honorable, there can be no doubt of that."

"That was understood all the time, my lord," Elizabeth murmured, "else I should not have come with you in the first place."

"Precisely," he said. He put his hand to his head for a moment as if in pain.

163

"If you have the headache, my lord, we can return inside," she said hopefully.

"No, this must be said, Miss Durant." He took a deep breath and turned toward her. "Elizabeth, I might say—I do not know why we have become so formal after all that has happened between us." He laughed shortly.

"No indeed, Ivor," she replied. "What is it that must be said?" she prompted after a brief pause.

"I am merely trying to think of how best to put this," he said, then smiled limply. "Elizabeth, when will you wed me? Properly, I mean; no more of this havey-cavey business for me."

"Never, my lord," she said promptly, and felt a great surge of relief in saying so.

He was plainly stunned. "But Elizabeth, we must be wed. I—you—you must allow me to do the honorable thing."

"I am afraid I must deny you that privilege, my lord, for I no longer have any wish to marry you," she said firmly. Now that the first refusal had been uttered, she had no hesitation in continuing in the same vein. "I have discovered that we should not suit at all. In a way, I am glad that all this has happened, for otherwise I might have discovered that unhappy fact too late."

"Well!" Westbridge huffed. Deep down inside he was relieved, too, but for the moment his wounded pride took precedence.

"Of course, I can count on you to breathe no word of this escapade to anyone, my lord?" Elizabeth asked anxiously.

"Miss Durant, I am insulted," he declared. "As it must be obvious to you that it is my sole desire to preserve your honor, if you will not allow me to do so by marrying you, I will certainly do so my holding my tongue about this whole little—escapade, I think you called it."

"Thank you, my lord."

164

"Miss Durant—"

"My lord, I believe we have nothing more to discuss. If you do not mind, I should like to return inside and see to Mr. Buckley's comfort."

"Of course," he said, and wordlessly they returned to the inn.

# THIRTEEN

When Elizabeth went upstairs to see Charlie, the three volumes of *Guy Mannering* under her arm, she found him asleep, Mrs. Currier keeping watch by his side. The goodwife assured Elizabeth that she would be there to do whatever was needful, so Elizabeth left the books on the side table and went off to seek her own bed. By the time Francesca joined her, Elizabeth was already fast asleep, and Francesca felt satisfied that all was as it should be, for tonight her cousin slept like a top.

As Nigel Foxmoor had had quite a long talk with Mr. Locke when he had met him in his club, he and Miss Locke were fully qualified to make an announcement of the most joyous nature the next morning. This engendered all the most tender feelings of motherly delight in Mrs. Locke's breast, as Emma repeated shyly some of the more stirring passages Nigel had used to woo her. So changed was this young lady by the love of a good man that she felt no satisfaction at all when Elizabeth mentioned quietly that it seemed both her engagements were broken off and it did not appear likely that she would marry anyone.

"Never mind, Lizzie," Emma said sympathetically. "You are still quite young yet, and you will find happiness like ours one day." She and Nigel exchanged rapturous gazes.

Francesca, too, added her reassurances, for she had little doubt that once Elizabeth told Charlie that it was all over between her and Westbridge, the final part of her plan would naturally fall into place.

Lord Westbridge himself had removed his disfigured and surly countenance from their company before breakfast that morning, and without his lowering presence and with the happy news from Mrs. Currier that Mr. Buckley had spent a restful night, the whole excursion began to take on the holiday spirit that Nigel had fully expected from the start. Mr. Foxmoor was even overheard to remark to Emma that Budgate was a dashed jolly place for a holiday and would she like to spend their honeymoon there?

Francesca and Richard Tanner were both eager to begin work on the program for her recital and asked Mr. Currier if he might know of anyone in the vicinity who would allow them the use of a pianoforte. They were recommended to try the rectory, where they were most cordially welcomed and indeed already felt as if they were among old friends. Mrs. Hopewell begged to be allowed to sit in on their practice, and was invited to make herself comfortable in a chair in the corner, where she occupied herself with her knitting. Richard Tanner was not an accomplished pianist, but he at least had enough skill to take Francesca through a few scales.

"Splendid, Miss DelSorro, splendid!" he cried upon hearing her voice. "I have rarely heard better, even in the great opera houses of Rome. When we return to London I am sure Luigi Bruno will jump at the chance to have you as his student."

"Thank you," Francesca replied, accepting the compliment as no more than her due.

After a few more minutes of scales, Mrs. Hopewell nodded off in her corner, and Richard took the opportunity to ask Francesca how her plans were progressing.

"I cannot help but think it will be difficult for you to win Lord Westbridge's heart now that he has removed himself from our company," he said.

167

"On the contrary!" Francesca declared. "Do not you English say that absence makes the heart grow fonder? I am sure this must be so, and if it is, Ivor will be that much more pleased to see me after we have been parted for some days."

"But how can you be sure?" he pressed her, feeling certain there must be some flaw in her argument.

"Have I not been correct about everything else?" she asked with unflappable confidence. "Look at Nigel and Emma, for instance."

"Was that your doing, too?" Richard asked with some disbelief.

"Partly," she admitted with becoming modesty. "I merely let Emma believe that she was stealing him away from me, which makes her victory all the sweeter to her. She is quite a changed girl since her betrothal. For Nigel's sake, I hope the change lasts."

"I did not know the lady before, so I can make no comparison," Richard said, "but I will say she seems very happy in her betrothal."

"Of course she is," Francesca said. "And soon Elizabeth will be just as happy with Charles, and will have no reason to accuse me of stealing Ivor away from her."

"Quite right," Richard said shortly, then, noticing Mrs. Hopewell's renewed attention, he cleared his throat. "Have you given any thought to what you will sing, Miss DelSorro?"

"Oh yes. After taking your suggestions into careful consideration, I have decided to do the aria you recommended from *The Barber of Seville,* as that is so popular now, and perhaps something by Mozart. I am fond of *The Magic Flute,* but do not care to sing in German; it is such an ugly language. What do you think of an aria from *The Marriage of Figaro*?"

"A very good choice," he said.

"I would also like to do a Spanish folk song, in honor of my native country," Francesca continued. "Perhaps I can sing that between the two arias. And of course I must finish with 'Greensleeves.' There is not an Englishman alive who is not exceedingly sentimental about that song, and it always produces the most tender emotions in the listener's breast. Even if he is a man without much sympathy for music in general, he cannot help but be moved by a feeling rendition of 'Greensleeves.' "

"I will take your word for that," Richard said dryly. "At least I am certain my pianist friend will know it, for no repertory is complete without it."

"Indeed," Francesca agreed happily. "And I will sing it beautifully—after I have learned all the words, that is."

"Then let us not waste any time!" he declared. "Even *my* limited repertory includes 'Greensleeves.' " And he pounded it out for her, happy to see that she was not led astray by a number of misplayed notes. He joined in with her where she was unsure of the words, and soon even Mrs. Hopewell was singing along quite happily.

While this musical interlude was taking place elsewhere in town, Elizabeth had gone upstairs to keep Charlie company and perhaps read to him as promised. She found him alone, lying in a darkened room, staring at the ceiling.

"How are you feeling today?" she asked gently, as she plumped up his pillows and helped make him more comfortable.

"The doctor says I will live," he said with a weak grin, "so I suppose I must believe him. I am glad to see you, Lizzie, I was feeling a little lonely. I have just been lying here, thinking."

"Brooding, more like," Elizabeth said severely. "It cannot be good for your health. Do you mind if I open the draperies? I can hardly make you out in the darkness."

"Go ahead, I expect the light will hurt my eyes at first, but I will grow used to it, as I have grown used to the pain in my head." He gave a martyred sigh.

"Pooh," Elizabeth said, moving over to the window. "If you think I am going to be taken in by that obvious bid for sympathy, you are much mistaken. There now,

169

that is better." She moved a chair over so she could sit near him. "Mr. Tanner has been kind enough to lend me a book to read to you." She picked up the first volume from the side table. "Do you think you would like that, or are you too weak to listen?"

"What is the book?" Charlie asked, with rather more interest than might be expected from one who professed to be at death's door.

*"Guy Mannering,"* Elizabeth told him.

"At last!" Charlie said. "I gave that book to Richard myself over a year ago with the proviso that he must loan it to me as soon as he was finished with it. It has certainly taken him long enough."

"Well, you can take him to task yourself, for he promised to visit you later on. Right now he is otherwise occupied. He and Francesca are planning a recital."

"A recital?" Charlie asked. "What is Dick going to recite?"

"He is not going to recite at all. It seems that Francesca is a singer and wishes to display her talents for us all. So you see, you now have something to get well for."

"I will reserve judgment on that until I have heard her sing," Charlie said. Then, after a pause while Elizabeth arranged herself comfortably to read to him, he said in a questioning voice, "Lizzie?"

She looked at him nervously, not at all comfortable with his change in tone. She would prefer to keep things light and impersonal between them until she had a chance to sort out her own future. "Yes, Charlie?" she replied.

"I hope I haven't ruined things completely for you."

"What do you mean?" she said guardedly. For a brief, hopeful moment she thought he might be referring to their own engagement, that things still stood the same between them, but this hope was quickly dashed.

"You and Westbridge," he said. "I hope I haven't destroyed anything between you."

"No, of course not," she murmured, her head down, but could not bring herself to add the vital stipulation

170

that there had been nothing to destroy in the first place.

He released his breath sharply. "Good. I mean I am glad for you. You are quite sure the two of you have come to an understanding?"

"Yes, we have come to an understanding," Elizabeth replied quite truthfully. "He left early this morning, you know, but we had quite a long talk after dinner last night."

"You don't know what a load that takes off my mind, Lizzie," he said. "I have been lying here thinking that I had ruined your life completely and that you would never forgive me for it. Of course, if you had come to me first—as you said you would—I never would have gone haring off after the two of you in the first place."

"I know, Charlie, it was wrong of me—but it all happened so quickly."

"Yes," he said, "I think I know how those things can be." He forced a cheerful smile to his face. "I think you will make a splendid duchess, Lizzie."

"Duchesses are not called Lizzie," she replied tartly, then, softening again, "But Charlie, I do want to thank you for coming after me. I mean, I know it all ended in a big muddle and it probably would have been better if you had remained safely at home, but nonetheless it is nice to know that you cared enough. . . ." She trailed off.

"Speak no more of it, Elizabeth. As I said, now that I know you and Westbridge are reconciled I can rest easy."

"Yes, we are reconciled," she said softly.

"And I hope all misunderstandings between you and me are cleared up as well."

"I hope so, too," Elizabeth said, even though she knew quite well they were not. But what could she say? Charlie was in a precarious state of health, and if it soothed him to think that she and Westbridge were still betrothed, why should she disabuse him of the knowledge? She was certain he could have no real

171

personal interest left in the matter, and she was determined not to provoke his pity again.

"Then I can look forward to dancing at your wedding?" he asked.

"For that you must get well first," she said. And I must find a husband, she thought. "May I begin?"

He nodded and settled himself into the pillows.

She opened the book to the first page. " 'Chapter one,' " she read. " 'It was the beginning of the month of November, when a young English gentleman, who had just left the university of Oxford, made use of the liberty afforded him to visit some parts of the north of England. . . .' "

It was when they were dressing for dinner that evening that Francesca learned her months of planning for Elizabeth's future were still not ended.

"I am glad to hear that Charles is so much improved," she said to Elizabeth as Conchita dressed her hair.

"Too much improved," Elizabeth said with a laugh. "At luncheon he threw his bowl of soup against the wall and demanded more substantial fare. It made a fearful mess, but I think he felt better for it. And Mrs. Currier didn't seem to mind a bit, for he presently consumed a large plate of beef and mustard, which somehow justified his destructive act. The doctor says he will be well enough to come down for dinner tomorrow night."

"Ah," Francesca said. "You must be happy about that."

"Of course," Elizabeth said, adjusting her sash in the wardrobe mirror. "But Francesca, I have a most important favor to ask of you." She glanced at Conchita, and Francesca, her hair dressed to her satisfaction, dismissed the girl.

"What is it, Elizabeth?" she asked with concern. "You know I would do anything for you."

Elizabeth sat on the edge of the bed and faced her cousin. "Charlie believes—or rather, I let him believe—that I am still engaged to Lord Westbridge. It seemed

172

to distress him to think that he had destroyed my chances with Ivor, and so I have told him that we are still betrothed."

Francesca was plainly displeased with this information.

"I know it is deceitful of me," Elizabeth apologized, misinterpreting her cousin's displeasure. "But at least until he is fully recovered I think it would be best to let him continue in this belief. I don't want him worrying about me, you see."

"And then?" Francesca asked.

"By the time I tell him the truth he will be able to view this whole episode more dispassionately, I hope, and realize he has no responsibility for what has happened." She arose and began pacing. "Don't you see, Francesca? The last time he offered for me was when Westbridge had rejected me, and it didn't work out at all well. I don't want him to feel obliged to offer for me a second time, for the same reason."

"One never cares for pity when it is directed against oneself," Francesca murmured.

"Exactly," Elizabeth said, bowing her head. "I must leave Charlie free to live his own life, instead of worrying about me all the time. I have inflicted enough damage upon him."

"Very well." Francesca sighed. "I will do this thing for you, and if you like I will tell Mr. Tanner of it, too."

"Thank you, Francesca," Elizabeth said. "You have been a true friend to me, and I hope you will always remain so."

"Of course I will, Elizabeth," Francesca assured her, but for the first time she wondered if she really deserved such a compliment, and she repeated her misgivings to Richard Tanner later that evening.

"I swear I do not know what has gone wrong, Richard," she complained to her confidant. "Here are two people who love each other and yet they seem to be the only ones who do not know it."

"If they do indeed love each other, then perhaps it would be best to leave them alone," Richard suggested.

Francesca considered this fantastic idea, then rejected it. "No," she said, "for it may take years."

"Then you must allow it to take years," Richard persisted. "Content yourself with the knowledge that you have at least helped Elizabeth overcome her infatuation for Westbridge."

"Yes, of course," Francesca said, and the thought of Westbridge and his fate cheered her somewhat, although not as much as it should have. For she had felt the first doubts about her ability to manage events to her liking, and if she had been mistaken about Charles and Elizabeth, could she not also be mistaken about Ivor? And then what was to become of her? She would return to Spain a broken woman and marry Don Carlos and his olive groves and arthritis. No, her plans *must* come out right, and she practiced "Greensleeves" until she could have sung it in her sleep.

"Where did we leave off yesterday?" Elizabeth asked the next morning when she joined Charlie in the inn's kitchen garden.

He had convinced the doctor that he would improve more rapidly if he were allowed some fresh air, and while the doctor had grave doubts about the efficacy of the same, he had no doubt that his patient was becoming most truculent and therefore should be allowed this liberty. "For there is nothing so contrary as an impatient patient," he said with a chuckle to anyone who would listen.

"We were up to the part where they sighted the smuggling lugger off the coast and the chaplain had come home without the little boy," Charlie said.

"You have lost the marker—have you read on ahead without me?" Elizabeth asked indignantly. "In that case, you will simply have to wait until I have caught up with you."

Charlie grinned sheepishly. "I did try to read on ahead, for I thought you had left off at a particularly stirring passage, but I am ashamed to admit I got nothing but a blistering headache for my troubles."

"It serves you right," Elizabeth said with a smile. "And I did not choose that passage to leave off, you simply fell asleep then. Ah, here we are." She cleared her throat and began to read. " ' "Mr. Sampson's been at hame these twa hours and mair, but I dinna think Mr. Harry cam hame wi' him." ' "

"Liz—Elizabeth, you needn't do the Scottish accent, you know," Charlie interrupted.

"But it is written that way," she protested.

"Yes, but the way you read it, it sounds Irish and is most distracting."

"That is gratitude for you!" she exclaimed, injured. "Here I am, reading you this great, silly book with all its gypsies and smugglers and fortune-tellers—trying to read this book and keep a straight face at the same time, and all you can do is complain about my accent!"

"You needn't keep a straight face, you know," he told her seriously. "It is *supposed* to be an amusing story."

"And if I did not fear that reading to you forever would be my punishment, I would rap you soundly on the other side of your head with it!" She laughed. "And you needn't put on that woebegone countenance, either. I know when you are play-acting."

"Pax!" he cried. "Read the story. I am all aquiver to know what has befallen the hapless Mr. Harry."

"Very well, I shall continue, and I shall give it whatever expression I see fit."

"I will try to bear it," he said, with a long-suffering sigh.

But even while they joked and laughed together like this, Elizabeth felt uncomfortable with him and was again reminded of her own unworthiness. What had happened to her steadfast resolve never to cause him another minute's pain? She could not even converse with him for five minutes without beginning an argument or taking exception to something he said. And yet he remained so patient and understanding, allowing not one word of reproach to pass his lips. She would be glad when his period of convalescence was over and they could return to London, never to meet again, for the strain of not throwing herself at his feet and begging for his love, however tinged with pity it might be, became greater as the days wore on.

In the meanwhile, though, it was no more than her duty to keep him company, reading to him every morning, playing whist or some silly parlor game with him and the others every afternoon, and making lighthearted conversation with him after dinner every evening, all the time keeping a tight rein on her emotions. The company was delighted to notice that Charles had become something of a local celebrity, and when he and Elizabeth were invited to take tea with the Hopewells along with the other two young couples and Mrs. Locke, their progress down the high street was greeted with the cheers and shouts of the local schoolboys for their hero, Blond Charlie. From what he was told, Charles began to wonder how anyone had won any money on him from the fight, for everyone he met claimed they had placed their bets on him—no one wished to admit to supporting a loser.

Finally, at the end of a week's time, Charles was pronounced fit to travel, and while they had all enjoyed their stay in Budgate, with its homely pleasures, not one among them was sorry to return to London.

# FOURTEEN

Elizabeth reentered the social rounds of London reluctantly. She had had much opportunity to think during her week in Budgate and had used that opportunity to take stock of her life and her prospects. As for her life, she saw now that it had been spent to no better purpose than seeking her own pleasures and gratifying her own desires. It was no wonder Charles Buckley pitied her, she thought, and now she pitied herself and in her momentarily heightened awareness realized that even this self-pity was nothing more than another selfish indulgence.

As for her prospects, she made a visit to her solicitors to discover these. She was satisfied that when she came of age in another year her income would be sufficient to support her in her own establishment, with enough left over to pay the wages of a suitably respectable elderly female to keep her company. What little was left after that she would perhaps put to use in doing good works. Her desire to reform her ways was strong, and she could think of nothing that would serve that purpose better than to devote her life to acts of a charitable nature.

She spoke nothing of her plans to her former confidante, and Francesca was greatly disturbed by her cousin's unnatural silence and air of resignation. She spoke of her worries to Richard Tanner after one of her morning practice sessions with Luigi Bruno, the great teacher of voice.

"Charles has not called on us since our return a week ago," she said, a distracted frown upon her face. "Apparently he still believes Elizabeth is betrothed to Ivor. How can I undeceive him of this notion?"

"I do not see that any action on your part is necessary," Richard said. "He is bound to find out for himself sooner or later."

Francesca was plainly horrified by this suggestion. "I couldn't allow that to happen!" she exclaimed. "He is bound to find out in a most unpleasant manner. I must be assured of a happy conclusion, else all my efforts will have been in vain."

"There is nothing you can do at the moment," Richard insisted. "I have seen Charles several times at our club, and he is still recovering from his injury and goes about very little. Once he is fully restored to himself, I have no doubt he will come to visit Elizabeth, and certainly it is she who should tell him that she is not engaged to Westbridge, don't you think?"

"I suppose you are right, Dick." Francesca sighed, taking his hand briefly and giving it a grateful clasp. "You are a pattern of good sense. Still, I cannot help but think there must be something I can do to speed things along."

But try as she might, she could conceive of no new plan to bring her cousins together again. Elizabeth had become distant and unreceptive; Charles she never saw. And in addition to preparing for her recital, to be held at the end of the week, she had other worries of her own. She had learned that when Westbridge had left Budgate he had gone on to Westham Park instead of returning to London. That in itself was no cause for alarm, for he would not have wished to show himself in town with a broken nose and two black eyes. But surely he must be presentable by now—and yet he had not returned. What if he did not come back in time for her recital? What if he remained in the country for the

178

rest of the season? Don Carlos and his olive groves became more real to Francesca every day.

Her only support throughout this time of worry and indecision was the calm good sense of Richard Tanner. Every morning he brought Signor Bruno to Upper Grosvenor Street for her lesson, and more often than not sent him home alone and remained for tea. He gave her guidance and encouragement, applauded her rehearsals, found an excellent accompanist for her, and even once lifted her spirits by presenting her with a lovely book of illustrated librettos. Francesca was also happily surprised to learn at an evening party that he was quite a good dancer and unhappily surprised to learn that he attracted the admiration of a number of other young ladies, for she had begun to think of him as her own personal property. It came as a very great surprise indeed to discover that he was considered a catch, for she had first met him only as Charlie's tutor and did not know that he had a small fortune and a well-respected family seat in the north.

The day before the recital Francesca was relieved of one of her worries, for she received a brief note from Lord Westbridge acknowledging her invitation and telling her to expect him.

"I cannot tell you how happy I am," she said excitedly to Richard, who, unfortunately, was unable to share her enthusiasm. "I was beginning to fear that he did not wish to see me again, after all that has happened, but he said in his note he is looking most forward to it and has something most particular to say to me! That can only mean one thing that I can think of!" She allowed herself a brief sigh of rapture. "Let us practice 'Greensleeves' one more time today, Dick. I want to be quite certain those high notes are sweet enough to melt his heart."

At least a few hearts were melted by her expert rendition of that song the following afternoon, and if Lord Westbridge's was not one of them, it was through no fault in technique on Francesca's part.

Ivor had entered the Lockes' drawing room hesitantly, wondering if he had been right to accept the invitation at all. However, Francesca had been a friend to him, and although he had resolved never to follow her advice again in the future, he still retained some tender feelings for their friendship and wished to tell her a very important piece of news that he was sure would interest her.

A small shadowing under his eyes was the only evidence of his recent injuries, and upon inquiry he told Mrs. Locke that he was quite recovered.

"Dear Francesca will be so pleased to hear it," she said. "She was most concerned that you would not be well enough to attend today, my lord."

He smiled slightly and told her he would not have missed it for anything. Then he noticed Miss Durant and Mr. Buckley talking together and, squaring his shoulders, made so bold as to approach them.

Elizabeth had not seen Charles for two weeks, but it was impossible for her to tell him how much she had missed him. Instead, she merely asked politely if he was fully recovered.

"I still get a headache when I read for too long," he told her. "I hope that does not last or I shall have to hire someone to read to me. Someone who can do a Scottish accent, of course," he added, hoping to draw a smile from her.

"I apologize for my inadequacies," she said quietly. The remark held none of the playful sarcasm she might formerly have used, but seemed to be a genuine expression of regret.

"What is the matter, Liz—Elizabeth? Isn't Westbridge treating you as he should? Do you want me to call him out again?"

Instead of laughing, as she was supposed to, Elizabeth merely gave him a bleak look and said, "Lord Westbridge has been in the country. I have not seen him since his return."

It was at that moment that Westbridge approached them, greeting each with a haughty bow.

"Miss Durant, so good to see you again. Mr. Buckley, I trust you are restored to health."

"Yes, thank you," Charles said, confused by Elizabeth's withdrawn reaction to her supposed fiancé. He gave her a sharp glance, but her eyes were downcast as she murmured something indistinguishable to Westbridge.

His lordship left them quickly when he saw his sister come in with the faithful Percy in tow.

"What is this all about, Elizabeth?" Charlie asked.

"Oh, why don't you leave me alone, Charlie?" she said sharply. "It isn't any concern of yours."

She turned and went to stand next to her aunt and Emma and greet the other guests.

Francesca's performance was greeted with delighted surprise by the audience, who had learned not to expect too much from these private recitals, which were often put on as a last-ditch effort to catch the girl a husband. But Francesca's voice was sure and sweet, and of a decidedly professional quality, and the songs she had chosen to perform were neither too long nor too short, but precisely of a nature to keep the audience paying full attention until they were finished, and perhaps even wishing she would go on. The piano accompaniment, too, was excellent, and a few listeners were moved to tears by her bittersweet interpretation of "Greensleeves."

Tea was served afterwards in the dining room, and it was a measure of Francesca's success that everyone present seemed to be in a good mood and disposed to linger long. She went through the crowd, accepting compliments on all sides, until she reached Lord Westbridge's side.

"El Colonel, I am so pleased you could come," she said, giving him her most brilliant smile.

"I would not have missed it for anything," he repeated to her. "I thought your performance admirable. You have met my sister, of course."

"Lady Imogen's was the first house I visited in London," Francesca said, including the lady in her aura of warmth.

"A very nice little show of talent," Lady Imogen said with a tight smile. "And if my brother enjoyed it, you must be quite certain it was a success, for he is most dreadfully tone-deaf and can hardly tell one piece of music from another."

"But I do enjoy listening to the words," he said quickly, noticing a small cloud appear on Francesca's brow. "Doña Francesca, I cannot remain too long, as we are expected at my father's for dinner, but I wonder if I might have a word with you alone."

"Certainly!" Francesca said, the cloud lifted. "If you will excuse us, Lady Imogen."

She and Ivor returned to the drawing room, which was now deserted, and she invited him to sit down.

"No, no, I cannot stay, and what I have to tell you won't take long, Doña Francesca." He smiled. "I only wanted to tell you, since you have been so kind as to express an interest in my affairs, that I am engaged to be married."

For once Francesca was bereft of words, and could only regard him blankly.

"Yes, I know it must be a great surprise, and so it is to me, too," he continued, completely unaware of her distress. "She is a lovely lady, a Miss Grainly. Of course, you have not met her as she has never been to London. Her father owns the estate next to Westham Park."

At last Francesca found her voice. "Congratulations, my lord," she said.

He smiled happily. "I particularly wished to tell you before the announcement appeared in the paper, for I have come to think of you as a very dear friend, Doña Francesca."

"That is most kind of you, El Colonel," Francesca murmured.

"And I do hope you will welcome Susannah when I bring her to town as my wife. She is very young, you see, and will be in need of a friend."

"Of course, I will be most pleased to meet her." Francesca gave him an automatic smile.

He took her hand in farewell and said, "I must leave now, as my father does not care for tardiness. I am sure I will see you again soon."

"Of course," Francesca murmured again and watched him leave. As soon as she was alone she gave a frustrated stamp of her foot and began swearing aloud in Spanish. If she had stopped to think, she might have been surprised to realize that it was not the loss of Westbridge in particular that vexed her so, but the fact that all her carefully laid plans had been well and truly spoiled by some chit from the country who, apparently, was no more than a schoolgirl.

Her swearing was cut short when she noticed Elizabeth run past the open doorway toward the stairway, with Charlie soon following in a less hasty but quite as determined manner. Francesca gathered her resources about her once more and decided that at least here she could do some good, but before she could follow them a strong hand gripped her arm.

It was Richard Tanner, who had entered behind her through the other doorway that led to the dining room.

"Richard!" she cried impatiently. "I must beg you to let me go! I am needed."

"Yes, you are, but not by Charles and Elizabeth," he said, leading her firmly to a seat.

"What are you doing, Richard?" she asked, struggling against him.

"I am preventing you from going where you are not wanted," he explained reasonably.

"But I must go to them, or are *all* my plans to come to nothing?" A few hot, quick tears of frustration came to her eyes, and she wiped them away impatiently.

"Do you mean you were not successful with Lord Westbridge?" he asked, releasing her at last.

"Not yet," she admitted, rubbing her arm. "Another obstacle has unfortunately been placed in my way."

"I see," he said with a slight smile.

"But no obstacle is insuperable," she said with deter-

183

mination. "Dick, perhaps you can advise me what to do—you know I have come to rely upon your good sense."

"I had hoped so," he said. "In fact, it was part of *my* plan."

She ignored his remark as she explained her new dilemma. "Lord Westbridge has engaged himself to some young girl from the country. How can I cause him to break it off and marry me?"

He sat down beside her. "That is indeed an obstacle," he agreed, appearing to give the matter a great deal of thought. "And I must admit it appears there is very little you can do, especially if the girl remains in the country."

"Yes, that is a problem," Francesca said. "I cannot turn her against Ivor if I have not even met her."

"You could write her a letter," Richard suggested helpfully.

Francesca looked at him suspiciously, certain he was making fun of her, but could detect nothing from his bland expression.

"While you are working on a way to solve your own problem," he said, "perhaps you can help me with one of my own."

"Certainly," she agreed readily, quite willing to change the subject for the moment, as the thought of Ivor's fickleness was beginning to give her the headache. "It is the least I can do for you, after all the help you have given me."

"Thank you, Francesca," he said, and then after a slight show of reluctance began his tale. "There is a lady I am interested in, but she is obsessed with another man."

"I see. Such a situation is always distressing. Does she love him—this man she is obsessed with?" Francesca asked him.

"No, I do not believe so, although she believes she does," he said. "In fact, I flatter myself by thinking she really loves me."

"Why, that sounds very like the problem I had with Elizabeth and Charles!" Francesca exclaimed.

"I suppose it does, but I do not think the same solution will serve. *I* have no knowledge of fisticuffs, and even if I did I doubt Westbridge could be persuaded to fight again."

"Westbridge? What has he to do with your problem?" Francesca asked, and then exclaimed "Oh!" as the truth occurred to her. "Do you mean to say that you are in love with *me*, Dick?"

"I don't know," he said, taking her hand. "As you are the expert on affairs of the heart, I was hoping you could tell me for certain."

"But I have done nothing to encourage you! I have not made a single plan to that end." She was slightly defensive.

"None were needed," he said simply, "except a few of my own."

"Oh, that is splendid!" she cried, suddenly throwing her arms about his neck. "I had no idea! I was always talking about Ivor, and you never seemed to object, so I was certain you had no interest in me. I didn't even *try* to engage your affections, for I thought it would be useless."

"You had no need to try," he said, returning her embrace, "for you had my affections from the moment I met you."

"Is it part of your plan to propose to me?" she asked presently.

"Certainly, if I am assured of an acceptance."

"Of course! To tell you the truth, I was growing rather weary of Ivor, for he hardly ever behaves as one expects, but I did not like to give up too easily. I kept remembering Don Carlos, who is a great friend of my father's and has many olive groves."

"I have no olive groves," Richard said apologetically. "But I do have a few wheatfields and even some cows."

"That will do," Francesca said generously. "It is too bad you are not a lord, though."

"My uncle is a baronet!" he told her proudly. "That is

almost as good as a lord. Of course, all five of my cousins would have to die before I came into the title. I am afraid you will have to be satisfied with my university title of don."

"That is quite all right!" Francesca told him happily. "Don is a most respected title in Spain. I can be quite content with that, especially as I do not approve of murder."

"I am glad to hear it," Richard said with feeling.

"Now tell me, Dick, is it in your plan to kiss me now? For I think I should like it very much."

"Anything to oblige, Francesca," he said graciously, and did as he was told.

Elizabeth could not bear it any more. If Charles gave her one more questioning glance, asked her one more time what was wrong between her and Westbridge, she would surely scream out in front of all the company. She had already avoided him twice, but when he approached her a third time, after seeing Ivor lead Francesca away, Elizabeth was certain he was prompted only by pity again. She could think of nothing else to do but leave the room and seek the privacy of her bedroom, where she flung herself upon the bed and waited for the sobs that were sure to come, sooner or later.

"I always knew I would recognize your bedroom by the heaps of clothing on the floor," Charlie said, kicking aside a few items as he approached her.

She gave a little scream of alarm and turned over quickly. "Charlie! What do you mean by following me up here? It is most improper!" She gave him a shocked look and then buried her face in her pillow again. "Go away, I don't want any more of your pity."

"Sorry, I can't hear you when you muffle your voice like that." He sat down next to her on the bed and touched one of her shoulders.

She reacted as if to a gunshot, scrambling quickly off the bed. "You must leave my room at once! If anyone should find us here together, what would they think?"

186

"That I would have to make an honest woman of you?" he asked with a small smile.

"Certainly not," she said, irritated. "I should not like you to feel that you have any responsibility toward me at all."

"Do not worry, I have not followed you with any intention of compromising you, but merely because you seemed to be in some distress and in need of a friend. Besides," he continued mildly, after his slight show of temper had died away, "you have spent a great deal of time in *my* bedroom; I do not see why I should not be allowed to visit yours."

"That was quite different," she said. "You were unwell and I was nursing you."

"And very nice it was, too, except that I thought you were engaged to Westbridge all the while." He stood up and faced her across the counterpane. "Why did you tell me that?"

"It was what you wanted to hear, was it not?" she said defiantly. "You were not well; if I had told you I had discovered that Ivor was an insufferable prig it might have distressed you."

"On the contrary, it would have pleased me no end, for I have been waiting for months for you to make that discovery. I am sorry, Elizabeth—"

"I told you I don't want your pity!" Elizabeth interrupted harshly.

He regarded her with confusion. "I have felt a great many things for you, Elizabeth, but pity was never one of them."

She turned away. "Then why else did you propose to me that first time if it was not because you felt sorry for me? There I was, miserable and rejected, the perfect object of pity."

"I see. If you felt that way at the time, why did you accept me?"

"Because I didn't feel that way at the time! I only realized it afterwards. Charlie, it is very noble of you to always be looking after my welfare, but there is no reason for you to sacrifice yourself on the altar of my

187

selfishness." She had become very fond of that phrase since the first time she had thought of it and welcomed this opportunity to say it aloud with great depths of emotion.

"The altar of your selfishness? What nonsense are you blathering, Lizzie? I assure you, it was not nobility that inspired me to offer for you, nor pity. Indeed, far from it—"

"You see, you are too modest even to admit it."

"Your view of me is quite flattering, but not at all realistic," he said with a slight shake of his head. "But I did not follow you up here with the intention of discussing my character, either. I wanted to know what went wrong between you and Ivor."

"Why don't you just go away and leave me alone?" she cried. "I am being smothered in your pity! It is quite obvious that we cannot be together for five minutes without arguing, and you deserve better than that. You needn't worry about me any more, you know. I have decided that as soon as I come of age I will devote all my time and money to charitable works. I hope that way to atone for my previous life of dissolution and dissipation."

She had addressed these proud remarks to the wallpaper and had not noticed Charlie inching around the bed behind her. Thus when he laughed the sound was quite close to her ear and caused her to start violently.

"I assure you, Charles, I am quite serious about this," she said, regarding him with what dignity she could muster.

His laughter faded as he searched her face. "Yes, I can see you are. I am sorry, Liz—Elizabeth. I had hoped— I should have killed Westbridge while I had the chance," he finished with feeling.

"What difference would that have made?" Elizabeth asked.

"None, I suppose. If you are going to carry a torch for him you can do it just as well whether he is alive or dead."

She opened her mouth to protest, then closed it again

188

and bowed her head, deciding that it might be better to let him continue to believe that than to learn the truth. At least it would make their separation easier for one of them.

"Well, Elizabeth, let me at least wish you luck in your endeavors," he said, taking her hands. "I wish my own future were as clear to me."

He leaned forward to kiss her on the forehead, just as she lifted her head to reply to him. Thus their lips met, and while they each opened their eyes wide with surprise, they did not break the embrace off immediately. Instead, Charlie drew her closer and applied himself more diligently to the exercise as Elizabeth welcomed his attentions and returned them with equal fervor.

In another minute, without quite realizing how the feat had been accomplished, they had tumbled onto the bed together, and they pursued their occupation there for some minutes, until Elizabeth broke off with a giggle and said, "Charlie! The door is wide open! What if someone should walk by?"

"Then I *shall* have to make an honest woman of you, make no mistake." He made no movement to rise and close the door, but kissed her again. "Now tell me, Lizzie, was there any trace of pity in that?"

"No," she admitted, "it was very well done."

"As well done as Ivor's famous kiss?"

The blissful expression left her face at once, and she pushed him away and stood up, smoothing out her dress.

"Really, Charlie, I think you had better leave at once. I don't know what came over us."

He sat up and grabbed her arm roughly. "I know what came over me! An intense desire to squeeze that brute out of your brain forever! Lizzie, can't you see that I love you to distraction? But what hope have I when you are always thinking about that bloody Ivor?"

"I was not thinking about him! *You* were the one who brought him up. I have not thought about him for a fortnight. Indeed, how could I, when I spend all my time thinking of you?"

"Truly?" he asked hopefully.

"Charlie, please do not look at me with that puppy-dog expression; it does not suit you at all," she said. She reached forward and stroked his temple with her free hand. "Are you quite sure you have recovered from your injury?"

"Quite sure."

"Then why must you think I am constantly comparing you to Ivor? There is no comparison to be made. Why, he is quite ten years older than you, and whatever brief and boardlike kisses I may have received from him were ample evidence of that."

A slow smile spread across his face. "Are you trying to tell me that you prefer me to Westbridge?"

"Yes," she said, then, suddenly shy, "And I am also trying to tell you that even though it took me a long time to realize it, I love you, Charlie."

The puppy-dog expression she had so disliked had now disappeared from his face, never to return again. "I have waited a long time to hear you say those words, Lizzie," he said, drawing her closer.

"Thank you for waiting, Charlie," she said.

"But I am afraid I will have great difficulty in living up to your new image of me. Somehow, I was always much more comfortable when you thought of me as rude and obnoxious and somewhat silly."

"Perhaps if you apply yourself, I can learn to think of you that way again," she suggested.

"I have no doubt of it. I remember many resolutions you made to reform your ways that all failed miserably."

She gave him a playful push. "There, you are already making progress."

"I was merely speaking truthfully, as my noble integrity directed me to," he said and laughed, but before she could retort again he stood up and gathered her into his arms once more. "I love you, Lizzie." He looked at her again, suddenly worried. "I may call you Lizzie, mayn't I? You are not going to be a duchess now, and it has been a great effort for me to remember to call you Elizabeth."

"I suppose I will have to let you," she said, then, so close to his ear that it tickled, "Do you know, Charlie, I rather think if you had kissed me sooner we might have avoided a good deal of trouble, for I find that I like your kisses exceedingly well. Would you mind very much kissing me again before we go back downstairs?"

"Not at all. I am delighted to discover something on which we can always be in perfect agreement."

"I suppose I will have to let you," she said, then, so close to his ear that it tickled, "Do you know, Charlie, I rather think if you had kissed me sooner we might have avoided a good deal of trouble, for I find that I like your kisses exceedingly well. Would you mind very much kissing me again before we go back downstairs?"

"Not at all. I am delighted to discover something on which we can always be in perfect agreement."